Mommy's Got You, Honey

Scarlett wasn't looking for a Mommy, but when she found someone who opened her up to a loving and supportive MDLG dynamic, she couldn't hide her ABDL side any longer

Tina Moore

Table of Contents

Chapter 1

"Dude, just take it. No one is even looking," Scarlett's friend Scott whispered to her as they walked through the aisles of the supermarket. Scarlett had been between jobs for the last two months, and it was starting to take its toll. She had enough money to pay for rent and a few utilities, but she had been losing weight as a result of not having any money left over for food.

This was typical of her life, three steps forward, and two steps back. Maybe it had something to do with the fact that Scarlett lived her life walking the line between right and wrong for as long as she could remember. It wasn't that she tried to be bad. It was just that every time she tried to be good, something bad would happen. She tried to make friends, and they would turn out to be into drugs. She tried to get a job. Her boss would bully her. She tried to do well in school. The popular kids would beat her up and spread nasty rumors about her. So in the 24 years that Scarlett had been on earth, she had learned to only depend on herself. The problem was, depending on yourself when you are between jobs can be somewhat of a tricky situation.

"I can't. The cops said that next time they catch me, it'd be jail time. You don't get it," Scarlett replied, pushing her hands in her pockets. She watched as Scott boldly turned and swiped a large can of tuna from the shelves, putting it in the front pocket of his hoodie and shrugging his shoulders.

"It's not like we are stealing alcohol or candy or cigarettes. We are literally just trying to survive," Scott sassed, making Scarlett roll her eyes and continue to walk through the store toward the cold food section.

It was true. In all the time that Scarlett had known Scott, he had never robbed a family or an old lady. He only ever took things from huge franchises that he knew would be okay if a

90cent can of tuna or corn or something like this, was taken. Scarlett shrugged her shoulders as she felt the rumble in her stomach and picked up a packet of cheese.

"I hope you're ready to run," Scott said as he saw the store security approach them as they headed toward the door.

"Let's go," Scarlett reluctantly nodded before breaking into a sprint and sidestepping the security. They raced down the streets, dodging other pedestrians and feeling the wind in their hair, laughing as they reached the park and turned around to see that the security guard had stopped chasing them and was walking back into the store.

"Nailed it," Scott panted, slapping Scarlett on the back. She was doubled over and felt as though she was going to be sick.

"I wasn't sure I'd make it. I am so hungry I was worried my legs would give way," Scarlett said as she stood up and began to walk through the park, towards her apartment.

"Want to come in? I've got some bread. We could have tuna and cheese sandwiches?" Scarlett offered, a delighted Scott beaming at her.

"Sounds perfect!" He exclaimed as they walked out of the park and onto the street.

"You there, stop," Scarlett heard an angry male voice as she was grabbed and pushed against the side of a brick building.

"You're under arrest. You have the right to remain silent," the male voice boomed as Scarlett saw Scott take off down the street, looking back in distress as he saw Scarlett being frisked before being pushed into the back of the police car.

That was two years and fifty-one weeks ago. Scarlett had successfully stayed out of trouble in jail of all places by keeping a low profile and following the rules the top dog demanded. She had even found herself a girlfriend who had some status, so for the most part, everyone had left Scarlett alone.

"Hey baby," Ross, Scarlett's girlfriend, said as she walked into the yard. Scarlett knew the drill. She walked over to Ross, kissed her passionately while letting Ross grope her before sitting on her lap and being put on display. Scarlett didn't really care. She had seen what happened to girls who didn't have the protection. They either ended up being used as mules for the top dog and all her friends or by the guards as fuck dolls. Both choices, Scarlett found to be less pleasant than being Ross's plaything.

"Hey, Daddy," Scarlett replied. Ross had told her that's what she liked to be called. Apparently, it turned Ross on and made her feel tough, but it did nothing for Scarlett.

"You're getting out in a week, aren't you?" One of the women standing around them asked.

"Yeah, we will have to see about that," Ross replied before Scarlett had a chance to speak. Ross cupped Scarlett's pussy predatorily while she sucked her bottom lip before slapping Scarlett's thighs and standing up behind her.

"See you later. I have some things I need to do," Ross said to Scarlett before she walked away, her friends following and leaving Scarlett standing alone in the yard. It didn't bother her, but as she looked around and up to the warden's office, she couldn't help but notice the warden looking down on her.

Fucking creep, Scarlett thought to herself before going back inside and heading to her cell.

"D block, showers," a guard aggressively yells as he walks down into the seating area. As the women start to file down the stairs, Scarlett looked for Ross. Usually, Ross made sure she got to shower with Scarlett and would find her along the way to the shower block, but as Scarlett approached the block, Ross was still nowhere to be seen.

Scarlett walked into the shower block. She noticed Ross leaning against the wall.

"Hey, baby girl," Ross almost snarled. Scarlett tilted her head, surprised at the venom in Ross's eyes as she felt a blow come down on the back of her head. Falling to the ground, Scarlett felt the kicks on at least four of Ross's friends as they stomped on her body and kicked her until she was a wailing mess on the floor. Ross snapped her fingers, and they stopped, leaving Scarlett writhing on the floor, clutching her stomach.

"What the fuck, Ross?" A guard grunted, picking Scarlett up and glaring at Ross. Not because he was annoyed that Scarlett was hurt, but because now he had to explain it to the warden.

"What, she slipped," Ross said, shrugging her shoulders and walking into the shower cubicle. Scarlett was picked up under her arms and marched to the medical block, where the guards pushed her onto a bed.

"She fell," one of the guards said to the nurse who was looking unimpressed by the situation.

"Yeah, I see that," the nurse sassed, as she

closed the door behind the guards.

"What really happened, sweetie?" The nurse gently said as she began to disinfect the cuts over Scarlett's face and arms.

"I slipped," Scarlett whispered, making the nurse nod her head, understanding how the situation went.

"Alright, let's get you all fixed up then," the nurse practically cooed as she began to treat Scarlett.

Scarlett stayed in the medical block for a few hours before she saw the guards coming back.

"She's not ready to be taken back," the nurse said as the guards began to pull Scarlett from the bed.

"She's not going back. Warden said to put her into solitary to keep her out of trouble," the guard replied, tightening his grip on Scarlett's upper arm as she tried to pull away.

"I don't want to go in there," Scarlett yelled, the fear in her voice upsetting the nurse.

"Don't worry. You'll be out in a week. Think of it as a silent retreat before going back into the real world. Now move!" The guard bellowed, pushing her forward and out into the corridor. It felt like a blur to Scarlett as she was bustled down the corridor after corridor. The nurse had given her some pain killers that had made her sleepy, and as she was pushed into a small, dark room, she collapsed on the bed as heard the door slam shut.

Now what? Scarlett thought to herself as she closed her eyes and went to sleep.

"Scarlett," a woman's voice affectionately called, causing Scarlett to wake up. She had no idea what time it was, as there were no windows and, therefore, no natural light. The singular ceiling light was broken, and as she slowly sat up in darkness, she could feel that someone was sitting next to her.

"It's okay, Scarlett. I'm not going to hurt you. It's me, Warden Healy. But you can call me

Esther," Esther explained.

"Why are you here?" Scarlett softly asked, not wanting any more trouble. It was bad enough that she would have to spend the next seven days locked up here. She didn't need to make matters worst by the warden taking an interest in her.

"I wanted to make sure you were alright. We both know you didn't fall," Esther simply stated. Scarlett shook her head, seeing the door begin to open and shielding her eyes from the light.

"Oh, good. I was hoping that it wouldn't take you long to fix this light," Esther declared as she watched the repairman begin to set his ladder up and tinker with the light fixture.

"Why are you doing this?" Scarlett whispered, slowly taking her hand away from her eyes and looking at Esther. What she saw surprised her. Usually, Esther's hair was in a tight, slicked-back bun, her uniform impeccable and a look for sheer domination on her face. What greeted Scarlett was anything but dominating. Esther had her long brown hair out, the waves softening her face, which had a natural covering of subtle makeup. She wasn't in uniform. Rather she was wearing casual clothes, the type that you would comfortably wear around the house. Her eyes didn't try to pierce through Scarlett's soul either. They were kind, gentle, almost loving. Scarlett shook her head, feeling herself being drawn to the woman. Esther noticed how Scarlett's pupils dilated as she took her in, and she tried to hide a satisfied smirk. This was the reaction that Esther was hoping to elicit from Scarlett.

Over the last, almost three years, Esther had watched Scarlett. How she interacted with the other inmates, the types of activities she enjoyed participating in, and the way she would snuggle into her blankets when she thought no one was watching. But Esther was always watching, and if there was one thing Esther knew how to spot, it was a little. However, the risk of trying to start something with Scarlett was far too high, for multiple reasons. Firstly, it was completely unprofessional and an abuse of power. Secondly, it could put Scarlett at risk, and thirdly, she could lose her job over it. Not to mention, if Scarlett didn't reciprocate the feelings, it would be disappointing. Yet now, with Scarlett in solitary confinement and about to be released, Esther thought that the risk was justified.

"Thank you for fixing that," Esther said to the repairman as he tested the switch, turning the light on before nodding and leaving.

"You can go to, you know," Scarlett snarled. She knew that having the warden's attention could only ever end in disaster and wanted to be as far away from her as she could.

"I'll go, but before I do, I thought you might want this," Esther calmly explained, taking Scarlett's blanket from behind her back and handing it to her. Scarlett couldn't contain her excitement and reached out to take it and brought it close to her face, burying her face in it before looking at Esther fearfully.

"It's alright, I'm not asking for anything," Esther reassured Scarlett before standing up and walking out of the cell, closing the door gently behind her. Scarlett felt her stomach knot.

Nobody ever gives something for nothing, Scarlett sadly thought, not believing a word that Esther had just said. She lay on her bed, thinking of all the times that she had given herself to somebody unworthy.

Maybe she will be different. Maybe it might be nice to find someone who won't let you down finally, Scarlett thought as she closed her eyes as she drifted off to sleep.

Chapter 2

Scarlett fell asleep curled up in her blankie, only waking to the muffled sound of inmates yelling and bouncing a ball outside her cell.

Must be yard time, Scarlett thought as she rubbed her eyes. The room was still dark and cold from the night, and Scarlett was glad she had her blankie to wrap around her tightly. She uncurled herself from her sleeping position and stretched. It felt strange to be by herself. Strange in the sense that she felt safe for the first time, as though she didn't have to be on guard. Walking toward the wall, she found the light switch and turned it on, happy that she had control over that.

I guess it's the little things, Scarlett thought to herself, wildly aware that not all cells had a switch that the inmate could control. She blinked her eyes until they adjusted to the brightness of the room and felt her way back to the bed. Sitting down, Scarlett sighed again, shaking her head and beginning to cry into her hands. This was the first time that she had cried in three years, and the tears stung her eyes as they fell into her hands.

"Shh, there there, it's okay, sweetie," came a voice that made Scarlett freeze. Looking up, Scarlett saw the face of Esther looking back at her, and she fearfully looked behind her to see that the door to the cell was closed.

"How?" Scarlett began to say as she tried to pull away from Esther and wipe her tears away.

"You didn't hear me come in?" Esther asked, reaching out and wiping Scarlett's tears from her cheek. Scarlett hated herself for pausing for a moment to let her before flinching and moving back, sitting with her knees to her chest against the wall.

"No," Scarlett replied, glaring at Esther. Esther looked at Scarlett, with a look of amusement and desire in her eyes.

"What?" Scarlett aggressively yelled, annoyed that her body was craving the gentle touch of the woman sitting opposite her. Everyone knew that a guard's affectation was dangerous. It didn't take a genius to know that interest from the warden was even riskier.

"Nothing, I just can't believe that you'll be out of here soon," Esther replied, shifting closer to Scarlett.

"Yeah, thank fuck. I'm sick of this shit hole," Scarlett replied, making Esther laugh.

"Yes, I would be too if I had to live in here," Esther said, taking Scarlett by surprise.

Don't fucking do it. Don't do it! Scarlett internally screamed to herself, feeling the emotional pull toward Esther and hating herself for it.

"Well, I'm glad that you are up. Enjoy your day," Esther said, slapping her hands down onto her thighs before getting up, walking to the door but then turning and facing Scarlett.

"Can I get you anything?" Esther asked,

making Scarlett frown.

"No," Scarlett replied, annoyed that Esther was so seamlessly creeping into her mind. Esther winked at Scarlett before she opened the door, only to close it again, locking it and walking back down the corridor.

"I'm so fucked," Scarlett said out loud as she lay back down on the plastic mattress and closed her eyes shut, hoping just to sleep the day away.

Scarlett spent the rest of the day trying to build a routine. She did push-ups, sit-ups, planks, and squats. She took naps and tried to make her meals last for as long as they could. Yet, no matter how hard she tried, she couldn't get the image of Esther out of her mind. Never before had she spent any time thinking about her, and yet, within two days, Esther had become all she could think about.

Relieved when the run went down, Scarlett finished her dinner, curled up in bed, and wrapped her blanket around her.

"Another cold night," she said out loud, wishing that she was already free and on the outside.

"Fuck off," Scarlett yelled as she heard the door to her cell open, assuming it was one of the guards. They had a habit of making getting a good sleep impossible.

"That's no way a young lady should be speaking," Scarlett heard, smiling despite herself as she realized that it was Esther standing in the doorway.

"Oh, sorry, I didn't think it was you," Scarlett replied, having to shake her head once she realized what she had said.

"That's better," Esther remarked, delighted at the change in Scarlett's voice and tone once she knew it was her.

"What is it?" Scarlett replied. She had decided that as long as she stayed in solitary than having a fling with the warden couldn't do her any harm, and had been planning on how she was going to seduce Esther if she insisted on continuing her visits.

"I thought you might need a friend. It's a cold night," Esther explained, closing the door behind her but keeping the lights off.

"Couldn't you get in trouble for this?" Scarlett asked, feeling Esther sit down next to her. As Scarlett tried to get up, she felt Esther reach out and push her back down on the bed, making her gasp but comply.

"Good girl," Esther cooed, placing a soft stuffed toy next to Scarlett.

"I know you only have a little bit of time left with us, and I wanted to make that time special for you. I know that you are a baby, I can see it in your eyes," Esther said, making Scarlett blush. She was happy that the room was dark. The last thing she wanted was to give Esther the satisfaction of knowing she was correct.

"Whatever," Scarlett replied, rolling over just to feel Esther's hands on her body, rolling her back, so she was facing her. Scarlett whined and wriggled, making Esther smile, her noises moistening her cunt and giving her the predatory edge she loved to experience.

"Shh, don't fight Mommy, little one," Esther said, stopping Scarlett in her tracks. Her heart skipped a beat, hearing those words from Esther, and she froze, unsure of what to do next.

"That's what I thought. Now come on, come and cuddle with Mommy and let's get that little body all warmed up," Esther said, placing another big blanket over Scarlett and coming to lay down next to her. Scarlett hated herself for turning into face Esther, her perfume soft, and her touch melting. Esther held Scarlett close to her chest, smiling when Scarlett reached her hand up to touch Esther's breasts.

"Yes, good girl," Esther said, kissing the top of Scarlett's head and gently beginning to rock her. Esther snaked her hand down Scarlett's back, over her ass and around to her pussy, making Scarlett gasp as she was touched. She wasn't used to being taken so gently. Ross had always been so rough and aggressive, Scarlett found the emotions that came with Esther's tender touch startling.

"Mommy isn't going to hurt you. Not like that awful woman you've been letting fuck you for protection," Esther said, still gently cupping Scarlett's pussy over her pants. Scarlett bit her bottom lip and tried to move away from Esther, Esther only laughing and pulling her back.

"I said I was gentle, not that you weren't going to give me what I came for," Esther explained, the feeling of being used, painfully familiar to Scarlett. She wished that someone wanted her for her, and she closed her eyes tight, trying to fight off the heavy sadness in her heart that once again, someone only saw her as a plaything.

"Just get it over with then," Scarlett sighed, the hurt in her heart feeling more intense than she thought it would be. Esther began to rub her, putting her hand down Scarlett's pants and kissing her neck.

"It's no fun if you don't want it, I'll be back when you're more in the mood," Esther said, standing up and walking to the door. It's not that she was particularly cold or distant, but Scarlett knew that Ester was disappointed. Scarlett lay silent on her bed. She wasn't sure what she was meant to say.

I don't know if I like it more, her being here or her leaving me alone, Scarlett thought as she saw the cell door open, closing swiftly and leaving the room silent and in darkness.

Chapter 3

What the fuck is all this? How am I supposed to deal with it? Surely she could find someone to be with on the outside? Why does she have to make me so fucking horny? Scarlett thought to herself over breakfast. Her bruising was healing as it should, and she knew that she only had a few more nights before she'd be able to be released.

I don't want her to come back. She'll probably be really mad if I refuse her again, Scarlett thought, wondering how to put off fucking Esther.

It's not that she's ugly or something, but I just wish she wanted me for me. She only sees me as a fucktoy, just like Ross does, Scarlett continued to think, feeling stupid that for a moment she thought that someone would want her for her, not for the innocence that they saw in her. She had always thought it was strange that women seemed to get high off taking her. As though by ruining the innocent and vulnerable sides of Scarlett would somehow feed their rotten souls or something.

"I just want to go home," Scarlett said softly to herself, wishing that it would come faster. The thing about jail is that Scarlett had never felt safe. She knew that someone was always sizing her up that she couldn't trust anyone and that, evidently, even the people who were meant to protect her and were only interested in their own motives. She imagined what getting out would mean. Feeling the soft grass under her toes, the wind in her hair, and being able to close her eyes and know that nothing bad could happen to her filled her with hope and excitement.

"You look pleased with yourself," Esther said, opening her cell door and making Scarlett open her eyes.

"I was just thinking of what I'm going to do when I get out of here," Scarlett replied, moving over to that Esther could sit next to her.

"And what is that?" Esther asked, placing a hand on Scarlett's thigh, high enough to make Scarlett look at Esther with questioning eyes.

"How about you lay back and let Mommy look at you?" Esther knowingly said, pushing Scarlett down. Scarlett bit her bottom lip, deciding that letting Esther have her fun was a better idea than annoying her.

Sure, she's not your first pick, but she's okay, and she's been gentle with you so far. You might as well let her, Scarlett thought to herself as Esther pulled on her pants.

"These can come off. Oh, baby, they really did a number on you, didn't they?" Esther said, kissing the bruises along Scarlett's thighs, making her shiver.

"I fell," Scarlett said, a tear escaping her eyes.

"Yes, I know you did, princess," Esther replied, pulling Scarlett's panties down and quickly licking her slit and making her gasp.

"Sweet little thing," Esther said, parting Scarlett's pussy lips with her tongue and tasting her deeper.

"Shh, it's okay, baby girl," Esther cooed as Scarlett gasped and tried to pull away from her.

"I'll be gentle, don't worry," Esther said, pushing Scarlett back down and gently licking and teasing her. Scarlett had to admit, it felt more loving than anything she had experienced in here, and as she let Esther have her way, she closed her eyes and gave in to the sensations.

Sure, it's a bit of an abuse of power, but it still feels so good, Scarlett thought, arching her back and pushing Esther's head away as she came, quickly huddling in the corner and looking at Esther with a frown on her face.

"You don't need to be scared, little one. Mommy isn't going to hurt you," Esther gently said, opening her arms to Scarlett, who slowly moved into them. Esther held onto Scarlett until her body relaxed, and she began to snuggle into the neck of Esther.

"I want my pants back on," Scarlett whispered, making Esther smile.

"Here, baby girl," Esther replied, reaching down and putting Scarlett's clothes back on her body. Scarlett reached for Esther once she was dressed, and Esther smiled as she finally had a compliant Scarlett wanting and needing her embrace.

"Mommy has to go now, baby girl," Esther said, enjoying the soft whine that came from Scarlett as she affectionately pried her hands off her.

"Will you come back?" Scarlett asked, the desperation in her eyes and voice filling Esther with the feeling of power and domination she longed to feel.

"If you're a good girl and play with yourself for me, I'll be watching," Esther said, tilting her head to the corner of the room where a camera was recording.

"Okay," Scarlett replied, biting her bottom lip and watching as Esther left her cell.

Scarlett waited a few minutes before timidly reaching into her pants and touching herself. It was one thing to pleasure herself when she knew no one was watching. It was a different thing entirely when she knew that Esther would be looking. The last night of her incarceration would be that night, and she thought about all the things she would do with her freedom. Feeling a shiver flow over her body, Scarlett teased herself, hoping that it was only Esther who was watching.

I guess I'll get out of here and use the $15 I have for a bus fare to the city. Then stay at Scott's place for a few nights while I try and get a job, save up a bit and then get my own place and take it from there, Scarlett thought to herself, arching her back, annoyed her wrist wouldn't flex enough to allow her to hit her g-spot. The only thing that she wasn't looking forward to doing on the outside was the mandatory therapy sessions that she had 50 hours during her probation period. Thinking about that made her angry, which in turn made her stop playing with herself, getting herself out of the mood almost instantly. She rolled over to face the wall and closed her eyes.

She had been told to go to therapy countless times in the past, always deciding that it was better to keep her fucked up ways to herself. It wasn't that she thought what she kept secret was particularly bad, but it was something that she would rather no one know, ever.

Maybe Esther wants to continue this on the outside. Maybe I will finally have something that I want, Scarlett thought to herself as she opened her eyes on the day of her release. Esther had come back that night to say goodnight and for a cuddle, telling Scarlett that she would be released in the morning and that she was a good girl for following Esther's request to pleasure herself. Scarlett loved how it felt to allow herself to slip into little space, even at the shallow level that Esther seemed to bring out of her so easily.

Scarlett's thoughts were interrupted by the sound of the guards opening her cell door and telling her that her time was up.

"Pretty nice show you put on last night. Never had a girl submit so easily," one of the guards sneered, causing Scarlett to feel a knot in her stomach instantly.

Don't say anything, just get out of here, she said to herself, feeling her eyes well up.

How could she, the fucking bitch, Scarlett internally screamed as she was given her belongings, processed and suddenly outside the prison gates and looking out onto the street.

"Okay, so, fuck," Scarlett said out loud, feeling overwhelmed and wishing she had somebody to turn to. She turned around, looking at the big building, surprised that for a moment, she wished she was back inside.

At least I knew what the rules were, she thought, deciding that she needed to wipe Esther from her mind and focus on what she was trying to do.

Get your life back, that's the only plan, she thought as she walked out into the sun and tried to find the bus station.

Chapter 4

Scarlett decided that it was better just to let go of the idea that she and Esther would have anything to do with each other on the outside.

She could do what she wanted in there, that's not the sort of person you want to be with, Scarlett told herself as she walked up to Scott's front door. He had obviously done alright for himself, as she stood on his doorstep and waited impatiently.

"Hello?" A voice said, causing Scarlett to turn around, her eyes going wide as she looked at the beautiful woman standing in front of her.

"Oh, hi. I'm looking for Scott," Scarlett said, trying with all her might not to look at the woman's breasts in the tight, fluffy light pink sweater.

"You must be Scarlett," the woman said, opening her arms and pulling Scarlett into her. Scarlett held her breath and bit her lip, looking up at the sky and trying not to blush as she felt the woman's firm embrace.

"Yeah," Scarlett replied, slowly pulling away.

"I'm Emily. Scott's girlfriend, he mentioned that you would be staying with us for a while. He said that you two used to get up to all sorts of mischief and that you took the fall for him a few years ago," Emily said, taking Scarlett's hand and walking her inside, shutting the door behind her and giving her a moment to take in her new surroundings.

"Nice, huh?" Emily laughed, putting Scarlett at ease. Scarlett liked that Emily hadn't brought up the whole jail thing, she seemed to know how to talk without triggering her in any way, and that made Scarlett instantly like her.

"Scott is just out getting a few things, he should be back in about 30minutes or so," Emily explained, leading Scarlett through the house and to a guest bedroom. Scarlett didn't want to say that this was the nicest place she had ever been. She thought her silence and facial expressions made it clear enough.

"Do you want a shower? Sometime to unpack and relax? Tell me what you need, honey," Emily said, affectionately stroking Scarlett's arm and looking at her with the warm and lovely eyes that made her stomach knot and churn.

Scott is one lucky son of a bitch, Scarlett thought as she cleared her throat.

"Maybe a shower, yeah. I'd love to get out of these clothes. I kinda just want to burn everything and start from scratch," Scarlett replied, surprised that she was so open with Emily.

"Well, I can't let you burn them, but we can absolutely throw them out and get you some new things. Do you want to go to the shops with me tomorrow and we can get you everything that you'll need?" Emily said, stopping when we saw Scarlett sit on the bed, smiling up at her.

"Yeah, that'd be great," Scarlett replied.

She figured she'd just buy a few pairs of panties, that way she could continue to wash her clothes until she had enough money to buy new ones. Scott had told Emily that Scarlett was attractive, but he had obviously not seen her for a few years, because she was stunning.

I bet jail was hard for you, cutie, Emily thought as she looked into Scarlett's big eyes.

"Okay, enjoy your shower," Emily said, reaching into the cupboard and passing Scarlett a navy towel before turning and walking out of sight.

Scarlet walked into the shower, turned the tap on, and looked around the room.

Shit, this is so nice, she thought to herself, looking at the shower gels, shampoos, and conditioners.

He made it. I wonder how they even met, Scarlett thought as she tried to wash away three years of bad memories.

She heard Scott come home, smiling as she

wondered how he would look and what sort of person he was now. He had never visited, but they had talked on the phone while she had been away. Getting changed into her old clothes, she nervously walked out to see him standing in the living room.

"Hi," Scarlett timidly said, waving at him and relaxing once she saw his face light up.

"Scarlett!" Scott exclaimed, rushing over to her and bear-hugging her, making her laugh. He had changed. He had a beard, he seemed taller, and he wasn't that hungry kid she remembered. He was muscular, thick-set, and strong.

"Wow, you've changed," Scarlett said, taking a set back and looking at him.

"Yes, I know how to look after my man," Emily said, walking into the living room with a plate of meats and cheese, crackers and fruit. Placing it down on the table, she offered Scarlett a glass of wine.

"Oh, I um, can't," Scarlett said, blushing

but making Emily beam.

"Such a good girl," she said, passing Scott a glass before the three of them sat down.

"So, you've come pretty far from what I remember you being like," Scarlett said, breaking the silence that had fallen between them.

"Yeah. I met Emily at a bar two years ago. I was down to my last $5, and I just thought, fuck it, I'll just drink it and deal with the consequences later. And she saw me and hasn't let me out of her sights since," Scott said, gently placing his hand on her thigh. Scarlett nodded her head.

"So, what's your plan?" Scott asked, catching Scarlett off guard and making her roll her eyes.

"I just want to get a job, get some money, and get my own place. I haven't thought of anything past that because it's a hard enough plan to make work. Not many people want to employ a felon," Scarlett explained, making Scott laugh.

"I'm kinda tired, guys. Thanks for all of this," Scarlett said, grabbing a piece of fruit and standing up.

"Have a nice rest, baby," Emily said as Scarlett walked down the corridor and into the guest room. Closing the door, Scarlett lay on the bed and felt her eyes well with tears.

Oh fuck off, Scarlett thought to herself, trying to push the gentle touch of Esther out of her mind.

"So, what sort of style are you going for?" Emily said, making Scarlett laugh. She had never thought about her style before, and certainly not for the last three years.

"I can only get a few things, Emily," Scarlett replied, embarrassed that she still felt like a prisoner. Sure she was on the outside but, it's not like she could just go and do whatever it was that wanted or buy whatever it was that she wanted either. Emily looked at Scarlett and tilted her head.

"Baby, I might not have made myself clear. Scott and I are going to get you everything you need to set you up because of what you did for him," Emily whispered into Scarlett's ear, making her shiver. Scarlett wasn't used to people being this kind to her, especially without wanting something in return, and as far as Scarlett could tell, Emily wanted nothing.

"Oh, that's okay, I don't need so much stuff anyway," Scarlett replied, feeling embarrassed by the look Emily was giving her. It was a mix of disbelief and something else that Scarlett couldn't seem to work out.

"No, I insist. Give me these, and go and get all the things you actually need and want. If you don't, I will, and I might not choose the things you like, so off you go," Emily said, gesturing to go back onto the shop floor and pick out more clothes. Scarlett hated to admit that Emily caring for her, made her wet.

You can't fuck your mate's girlfriend. She is probably just being nice, and you just think it's something more because that's how you think. But it isn't, and she's just nice, Scarlett said to herself, not wanting to stuff up her situation. The last thing she wanted to do was ruin something good, just because she seemed to only attract people who wanted to use her. Scarlett ended up getting two outfits to wear for when she was applying for jobs, a selection of jeans, shorts, t-shirts, and sweaters, and a jacket. She got underwear, socks, and a few pairs of sneakers, a pair of ballet flats and sandals, as well as a pair of boots.

"This is really lovely of you guys, thank you," Scarlett said, as Scott helped unpack the car.

"No, dude, thank you. You could have ratted me out, but you didn't. I mean, I'm pretty sure that I would have been locked up as well after all my priors. This is the least I can do," Scott explained, making Scarlett's heart swell.

"Yeah, well, I was always looking out for your ass, wasn't I?" Scarlett joked as she walked inside the house, happy that her life seemed to be going in a positive direction for the first time in a very long time.

"How's the job hunting going?" Emily asked Scarlett as she came home late for the fifth night in a row. Scarlett exhaled loudly, made a dramatic collapse onto the couch and groaned.

"I swear, there is nobody hiring in this fucking city," she replied, smiling as she felt Emily put a blanket over her.

"Then have a little rest before dinner. Try not to stress about it, you'll find something," Emily said, stroking Scarlett's forehead. Scarlett hated when Emily was affectionate like this to her. It reminded her of everything that she wished she could have for herself.

Trust Scott to end up having the most beautiful, affectionate partner on the planet, Scarlett thought to herself pouting, before remembering that Emily was talking to her and was expecting a reply.

"Yeah, I'll try," Scarlett said, thinking about how the only thing worse than not having found a job yet was that fact that she had her first mandatory therapy session in the morning.

Scarlett sat in the waiting room of the therapist's office, wishing that the floor would open up and that she would be able to fall through and out of this situation. She hated shrinks. They always tried to make her issues seem like something they weren't.

"Scarlett," a woman in her late 30's called from the corridor.

Here we fucking go, Scarlett thought to herself.

At least my clothes are comfy, she added, walking passed the woman, not being able to miss the sweet and sensual scent of her perfume.

"Hi, I'm Rachel," the woman said, gesturing to Scarlett to sit on the couch. Scarlett looked around the room.

These rooms always look the same. Some

abstract art on the walls, office furniture, the feeling of being observed, she thought, picking at her cuticles.

"So, you're here for your mandatory 50 hours. Is there something that you'd like to talk about specifically?" Rachel asked, enjoying having a new client. Rachel had been a psychologist for the last 15 years, deciding that her passion for working with ex-cons was her calling.

"No," Scarlett replied, looking around the room. She hated to admit. Her shrink was gorgeous.

"I thought that might be the case. Well, you're here for an hour, you can sit in silence if you like or we can get to know each other a little bit," Rachel offered, tilting her head at the bottle of water on her desk and offering Scarlett a glass.

"No thanks," Scarlett replied, her guard up higher than she knew it could be. There was a difference between being tough in prison than being on guard in the real world, and Scarlett was feeling the difference.

"You go first then," Scarlett said, a glint of mischief in her eyes, she had already figure out what she was going to say to whatever superficial crap Rachel replied with and was excited about starting the game.

"Well, I'm 38, I have a dog called Henry, and I'm not married because I like having sex with all sorts of different people," Rachel replied, taking Scarlett by surprise and ruining her smartass comeback that she had planned.

"Cool," Scarlett replied, being taken aback and somewhat impressed.

"Maybe this could be fun after all," Scarlett added, enjoying the smug expression on Rachel's face.

"Don't be too quick to judge me, baby girl," Rachel said, noticing how Scarlett's eyes glazed over at the words.

"Don't call me that," Scarlett whispered, looking into her lap.

"Pardon," Rachel said, leaning forward to

hear better.

"I said, don't fucking call me that," Scarlett yelled, getting up and pacing the room. Rachel liked that she had hit a nerve, and was curious to find out why it pained Scarlett so much to be called that. Scarlett moved to the corner of the office, looking out at Rachel with hurt in her eyes.

"Want to tell me what happened?" Rachel softly asked, slowly walking over to Scarlett and reaching out her hand. Scarlett moved away, pushing Rachel's hand away, just for Rachel to continue.

"It's alright, honey," Rachel said, as she made contact with Scarlett. Scarlett flung her arms around Rachel, burying her face into the woman's soft neck and feeling her heart finally be able to have a break. It had been years since Scarlett had felt as though she was safe, and in the soft arms of the older woman, Scarlett didn't even care that this wasn't the right thing to do in a session. She was surprised to find herself holding the woman, feeling as though her heart was a hot coal, put into a bucket of water.

"I've got you, honey," Rachel gently said, walking Scarlett back to the couch and holding her, cradling her in her arms.

"I'm sorry," Scarlett said, smiling as Rachel placed her hand over her mouth.

"You don't need to say sorry, honey. That's what this is all for, for healing. You can cry," Rachel affectionately said. Scarlett hated herself for letting this woman see a side to her that almost no one ever saw. But what she couldn't shake was the feeling of surrender. Almost as if, if she just allowed herself to be nurtured by this woman, that everything would be alright in the end, if the hurt she carried with her ever ended.

Chapter 5

Scarlett left the session feeling more lost than she did before it, making her mad as she replayed what had happened.

She's going to think I'm so fucking weird. I can't tell her that. I just can't, Scarlett thought to herself. She decided it was better to find something she wanted to work on, so the topic of her sexual appetite didn't come up. Scarlett got the vibe off Rachel that Rachel would stop at nothing to uncover Scarlett's most private secrets, and that wasn't something Scarlett wanted to give up.

Everyone just uses it against you. It's like, they see the soft side and then want to ruin it or something, Scarlett thought, trying to regain her composure as she walked through the door and into Scott and Emily's house.

This is going to be a good day. I can just feel it, Scarlett continued to think, deciding that she was going to go out and try to find a job, this time not taking no for an answer.

"Hey, good news," Scarlett said as she walked into the next session. She hated that Rachel wore her hair down, making her instantly have to hold her breath. Scarlett knew what it was about Rachel that had her unnerved. It was her aura. The whole, Mommy vibe that she gave off. Her generous breasts, her long brown hair, her happy and gentle eyes and smile, and the way her clothes seemed snuggly and welcoming.

Just fucking stop it, Scarlett whined to herself, as she found herself looking over Rachel's body. Rachel noticed Scarlett's untrained gaze, enjoying that the outfit she had deliberately worn, had paid off.

"What is it?" Rachel said, sitting down and getting out her note pad.

"I got a job," Scarlett replied, crossing her legs on the couch. Rachel smiled and wrote something down.

"That's great. Is it something that you wanted?" Rachel asked, making Scarlett scoff.

"No. It's washing dishes. But the people who will willingly employ an ex-con are few and far between. I think I'm going to get some money together and then get a new job. Hopefully, I can keep my past from following me," Scarlett said, folding her arms across her chest.

"That all sounds really positive," Rachel said, putting her note pad away. They sat in silence, Scarlett looking anywhere but Rachel, amusing her.

"What is it?" Rachel asked, looking inquisitively at Scarlett, knowing exactly what had unnerved Scarlett.

"Nothing," Scarlett said with an attitude. Rachel thought for a moment before getting up and coming to sit next to Scarlett, instantly making her hold her breath.

"Well, this, this isn't nothing," Rachel said, referring to the way Scarlett tried to distance herself.

"What are you afraid of?" Rachel gently asked. Scarlett glared at her, angry that she could see past the cool and somewhat aggressive exterior that she thought she put up so well.

"Fucking nothing," Scarlett whined, annoyed that Rachel wasn't being deterred by her hostility.

"Tell me about your childhood," Rachel asked, remaining in her spot next to a cowering Scarlett.

"What fucking childhood. I was on my own for most of it," Scarlett said, frowning and not wanting to cry.

"Are you going to write that down in your fucking book?" Scarlett mocked, wiping a rouge tear that fell onto her cheek.

"No," Rachel slowly replied, looking at Scarlett.

"Scott was all that I had," Scarlett said, getting used to feeling Rachel so close to her.

"Do you want to talk about him?" Rachel asked, hanging Scarlett a tissue.

"There's not much to say. I took the fall for him, he got himself a lovely little set up in the best part of town with his gorgeous girlfriend, and I have to come here and talk about my fucking feelings," Scarlett angrily replied, bringing her knees up to her chest and feeling more alone than she knew she could feel.

"That's probably why I am so fucked up," Scarlett said, looking up at Rachel, with nothing but fear in her eyes.

The angry ones are always the sweetest, in the end, Rachel thought watching how Scarlett's fierce guard came down and her big baby girl eyes looked up at her.

"You wanna talk to me about it?" Rachel asked, smiling kindly down at Scarlett and making her roll her eyes.

"I can't," Scarlett whispered, wishing that she could say the words she so desperately wanted to say.

"Yes, you can," Rachel said, suspecting that Scarlett's big reveal was that she liked the

MDLG kink on some level. Rachel had been a Mommy Dom for long enough that she could spot a baby, or even a potential baby from a mile away. They all had a few things in common, that subtle look of longing in their eyes, no matter how much ego, aggression, or bravado they tried to mask it with. Scarlett was no different. Her whole, I fucking hate the world, but please love me, vibe gave her away the moment Rachel saw her.

"Is it that you want to feel safe?" Rachel softly asked, her eyes smiling as she saw Scarlett gently nod her head.

"Is it that you want, Mommy?" Rachel asked, Scarlett's eyes darting up to look at her, like Bambi in the headlights.

"It's more common than you'd think," Rachel said, soothing Scarlett's fears.

"I have to go," Scarlett said, wanting to get out of there, now that her secret was out in the open.

"You don't actually. There's still

25minutes left," Rachel answered, watching as Scarlett once again paced around the room.

"Fine," Scarlett said, sitting down again and refusing to look at or talk to Rachel until their time was up.

Rachel went home after a long day of thinking about Scarlett.

You know what you are doing, and you need to stop, she said to herself as she showered. The room was steaming up as the hot water poured over her body. She knew that she shouldn't, but Scarlett just made her feel so deeply.

She is in a vulnerable position. She's trying to get her life back. You can't do this to her. Just wait until she's finished her sessions and then, maybe, see if something could work, Rachel said, finding that her hand had slipped between her thighs, pressing her fingers into her as she thought about how it felt to hold Scarlett. Rachel hated herself for her predatory ways at times. She felt like a dirty, dangerous predator as she remembered how hot it had made her, making Scarlett to submit to her.

Just go out and find someone who is already down for this, she thought, knowing that she could have a playmate in seconds if she went online.

"But I want her," Rachel hungrily said out loud, her eyes opening and their dominance reflecting in the mirror. Rachel knew how to seduce Scarlett, but she also knew that she needed to do the right thing by her.

"Why are you like this?" Rachel asked herself in the mirror, half expecting a reply. She rolled her eyes and walked out of the bathroom into her bedroom and put on some loungewear. She went online, saw the different girls who were looking for an online play partner, but she soon put her phone down, and closed her eyes. Reaching into her leggings, Rachel smirked to herself as she replayed Scarlett's face and her moody attitude that subtle, untrained bratty behavior making Rachel wet as she thought about how she was going to turn her into her good girl. Rachel imagined tying Scarlett up, her arms behind her back as she groped her breasts, kissed her lips, and touched her pussy, making sure that Scarlett knew that she was owned.

"Mommy's good girl," Rachel imagined herself saying, moaning in sexual relief as she began to circle her clit and play with her own breasts. She imagined Scarlett, sticking her tongue out and tasting her for the first time, her sweet little lips pressed against Rachel's wet mound.

"Fuck," Rachel said out loud, opening her eyes and rubbing herself with a desperation that didn't seem to end.

"This isn't going to end well," Rachel moaned as she came, fully aware that what she wanted with Scarlett was forbidden.

"Woah," Rachel said as Scarlett stormed in for their next session.

"You know what is fucking bullshit?" Scarlett angrily said, looking at Rachel and waiting for her to reply.

"Tell me," Rachel said, pulling her cardigan across her breasts, distracting Scarlett for a moment before her rage found her once again.

"That everything is so hard," Scarlett said. She had been furious until she had seen Rachel, but something about her soft, loving way made Scarlett forget that she was angry. Rachel smiled as she noticed this as well, feeling herself slowly fill with desire.

"What's hard?" Rachel asked, tilting her head and licking her lips.

"Oh, just this online course I'm doing right now. I want to become a security guard," Scarlett calmly said, completely disarmed.

"I think that's a great idea. You'd love that a lot more than doing dishes," Rachel said, making Scarlett smile.

"Yeah, I know," Scarlett replied, sitting on

her hands and looked around the room. Rachel waited for the silence between them to settle before speaking.

"So, I was wondering if you'd like to try a different type of therapy with me?" Rachel asked, Scarlett's eyes curious and questioning.

"It's called cuddle therapy, have you heard of it?" Rachel questioned, Scarlett, shaking her head and wondering if this is just all she had needed all along.

"It's especially good if you don't have a history of physical touch, which is important to soothe the nervous system and maintain a healthy mental balance. There's a thing call touch starvation, and it can have negative side effects," Rachel explained. Scarlett clenched her calves and didn't really know what to say.

"I haven't heard of it," she decided on and waited for Rachel to make the next move.

"Would you be interested in trying it? Obviously, we can stop at any time?" Rachel reassuringly said, watching as Scarlett timidly nodded her head.

"Okay. I'm going to come over there and lay on the couch, alright?" Rachel said, standing up and slowing, walking over to the couch. Scarlett stood up and got out of the way, watching as Rachel lay down. Rachel pulled her hair out from her bun, letting it tumble down, and her cardigan opened, showing off her grey sweater, making Scarlett bite the side of her bottom lip.

"Do you want to come and lay next to me?" Rachel asked. Scarlett moved slowly into her arms and felt like she would burst into tears the moment she felt Rachel's arms wrap around her. Scarlett lay rigid, trying to keep her breathing regular but finding that her breaths were short and shallow, her heart racing.

"It's alright, Scarlett," Rachel cooed, beginning to stroke Scarlett's hair, smiling as she felt the younger woman cautiously being to relax. Scarlett hated that this felt so nice, she was uncomfortable with Rachel's caring touch and gentle ways. Rachel repositioned herself so that she was slightly over Scarlett and able to look down at her, seeing her eyes begin to well up.

"You're safe here," Rachel whispered, stroking Scarlett's frowning forehead, the fear in her eyes still present. Tears began to stream from Scarlett's eyes, her silent crying breaking Rachel's heart.

"Oh sweetie, it's alright, Mommy's got you," Rachel involuntarily said, smiling as Scarlett snuggled into her. Rachel hadn't realized that she was so deep in Mommy space, delighted that Scarlett hadn't tried to push her away, and in fact, snuggled in closer to her chest.

"Do you want to suck your thumb? Rachel affectionately asked, Scarlett's aqua eyes looking up at her and timidly nodding her head.

"There's a good girl," Rachel cooed, taking Scarlett's hand in hers and bringing her thumb up to her mouth, watching as Scarlett looked at peace for the first time since their sessions had started.

Chapter 6

That was so amazing, Scarlett thought as she walked out of Rachel's office and out onto the street. She felt light in her heart, her fears of being touched seemed to disappear, and she felt as though everything was going to be alright for the first time in her life. Rachel had held Scarlett's timid body, gently rocking her like a Mommy and patting her affectionately as she snuggled into her breasts, getting lost in the feeling of safety and love for an hour, smiling at her as she became more confident and soften in her expression and attitude.

Rachel had closed the door behind Scarlett as she left, feeling her wet pussy rub against her panties as she sat back down on her office chair and recalled how Scarlett had voluntarily closed her eyes and relaxed into her arms.

Oh, my sweet girl, Rachel thought as she replayed the image, rubbing her breasts and gently pinching her nipples as she remembered Scarlett's soft breath hardening them under her bra.

"Dude, what's up with you?" Scott asked as Scarlett floated into the house and crashed on the couch.

"My therapist is fucking amazing," she replied absentmindedly, her mind was still in Rachel's office, enjoying the feeling of somebody touching her without making her feel as though she owed them for their kindness.

"That's good," Scott replied, unsure of what the appropriate response.

"I'll be out of your hair in about three weeks," Scarlett called as she saw Emily come home with the groceries. Emily had taken to calling Scarlett, baby, and it had made her wet countless times.

"That's alright, baby, whenever you're ready. Come and help me with this," Emily said, putting the groceries on the bench and waiting for Scarlett to get up and follow her instruction.

"You know that Scarlett's a baby, just like you are right?" Emily questioned Scott as they got into bed that night. Emily had diapered Scott and put him in a dino onesie, before letting him in their bed and stroking his hair as he snuggled into her.

"Really?" He asked, putting his thumb in his mouth and grabbing at Emily's pajama top. Emily just smiled as she looked down on the sweet boy she had all to herself.

"Yeah. How would you feel about Mommy seeing if she wanted to stay a little longer?" Emily asked. She had fantasized about having Scarlett and Scott in each arm, both nursing on her as she cuddled in bed.

"No, Mommy, I want her gone in the three weeks she said she'd go so I can be little again. But you can be cute with her if you want," Scott pouted, making Emily smirk.

"Mommy's greedy little boy. Alright then,

I'll be cute with her," Emily replied, enjoying Scott's wording and continuing to think about how adorable she'd make Scarlett as she patted her baby boy to sleep.

Emily woke to the soft sounds of distress coming from the guest room, where Scarlett had been staying for the last two weeks. She slowly got out of bed as to not wake Scott, and quietly walked down the hallway, opening the door to see Scarlett having a nightmare.

Sweet baby, Emily thought as she saw Scarlett toss and turn. Walking into the room, Emily gently sat on the bed and placed her hand on Scarlett's chest.

"It's alright, sweetie, it's just a bad dream," Emily whispered, waking Scarlett up and looking around in a panic.

"Hey, there, honey. You're alright," Emily said, calming Scarlett, who was now able to focus her attention.

"Sorry, was I too loud? Did I wake you

up?" Scarlett apologetically said, blushing and bringing her knees to her chest.

"No, not at all," Emily replied, smiling at Scarlett and pulling her bedsheets back.

"Come on, let me tuck you back in and pat you back to sleep," Emily said, taking Scarlett by surprise.

"Oh, it's okay, you don't have to," Scarlett said, moving her body under the sheets anyway.

"Good girl," Emily said, pulling the sheets up around Scarlett and tucking her in.

"Roll over sweetie, onto your tummy for me," Emily said, happy when Scarlett obediently followed her instruction as Emily began to pat her back, putting her to sleep in no time at all. Emily had a firm touch, far firmer than Rachel had, and Scarlett replayed the gentle ways that Rachel had positioned her in their last session together.

I wish this was Rachel, was the last thing Scarlett thought as she put her thumb in her mouth just as she fell asleep.

Scarlett woke up the next morning, knowing that she had to go to therapy and trying to find any excuse to get out of it.

"Do you want me to wash your cars, or do we need something from the store, I can get it," Scarlett said over breakfast. Scott just looked at her curiously.

"No, we have everything we need. Don't you have therapy and work today?" He asked as Emily filled up their water glasses.

"Yeah," Scarlett replied, looking down and digging her fork into her pancakes.

"What's the problem?" Emily asked, taking Scarlett's fork and feeding her a mouthful, making Scott jealous.

"Don't look at me like that, baby," Emily said, the warning in her voice making Scarlett curious and Scott annoyed.

"I don't want to keep going to therapy, she is getting to know me way too much," Scarlett replied, jumping when Scott loudly threw his plate into the sink.

"Everyone has things they have to do even if they don't want to. Get over it," he loudly said, walking away into the bedroom, and leaving Scarlett looking confused.

"Don't worry about him. He's grumpy when I get the final word about something. That has nothing to do with you," Emily reassuringly said, coming over to Scarlett and placing her hands either side of her face and kissing her forehead.

"Go, it'll be good for you," Emily lovingly said, before following Scott into the bedroom and closing the door behind her.

I think I'll still give it a miss, Scarlett thought as she finished her breakfast and went to get changed.

Scarlett ignored the session reminder, the phone call, and text from Rachel, putting her phone in her back pocket and headed to the shops.

They might not need anything, but I need

a drink, she thought, only to remember that she wasn't allowed to drink until her probation was over.

This is fucked, she whined to herself, passing the liquor store and going to a corner shop, deciding to buy a packet of chips instead.

"Well, at least I know you haven't been run over," a voice said behind Scarlett. Scarlett froze, feeling like a naughty girl who had just been caught doing something she knew she shouldn't.

"Um," Scarlett replied, turning around slowly. Rachel looked different outside her office. She seemed to be taller, but somehow, even in her casual clothes, she looked domineering and strong. It was a different type of energy, one which Scarlett hadn't experienced before because as fierce and intense as Rachel was, the kindness and affection that seemed to flow from her made Scarlett's head spin.

"That's what I thought," Rachel said, taking the packet of chips from Scarlett's hands and walking to the cash register.

"Hey, I can buy these myself," Scarlett whines, hating herself for getting turned on by Rachel's wide hips and thick-set thighs.

Mommy, Scarlett, whined out of frustration and lust to herself, feeling her desire to be Rachel's center of attention, beginning to take her to a space she wished she could fight.

"I'm sure you can, but I think I need to remind you who is in charge. You do know that these sessions are mandatory. Meaning that if you don't come, you'll be in a lot of trouble. I haven't told anyone you decided to bail, but I'd like to know why," Rachel said, paying the cashier, opening the bag and passing Scarlett the packet.

"You make me feel weird," Scarlett mumbled. Rachel reached out and lifted Scarlett's chin until their eyes met.

"Pardon?" Rachel asked, raising an eyebrow and looking down at Scarlett.

"You make me feel weird," Scarlett

replied, her eyes looking fearful, the way that turned Rachel on.

"Well, let's go talk about this then," Rachel commanded more than said, wrapping an arm around Scarlett and leading her to her office. Scarlett smirked to herself as they walked.

This is the start of so many porn videos, she thought, enjoying her chips and Rachel's firm but gentle embrace.

Rachel sat in her office chair and looked at Scarlett, sitting across from her.

"Talk to me," Rachel said, Scarlett beginning to pull at her cuticles.

"It felt weird when we hugged and stuff," Scarlett softly said, beginning to blush. Rachel had tied her hair into her signature bun, showing off her collar bones and model-like neck. Scarlett could almost detect the faintest of smirks coming over Rachel's face.

"Weird good or weird bad," Rachel asked, fighting her urge to sit next to Scarlett.

You just need Mommy, don't you baby, Rachel thought, eyeing Scarlett.

"Weird good," Scarlett softly said, annoyed at herself for feeling like she was falling into little space as she fidgeted with her fingers.

"Then come here," Rachel replied, taking Scarlett by surprise as she patted her lap. Scarlett slowly got up and made her way across the room.

"This isn't like, normal therapy is it?" Scarlett said as she felt Rachel's hand on her wrist, pulling her down and smiling as Scarlett wrapped an arm around her shoulders.

"Why would I give you 'normal' therapy? You told me that you didn't need therapy, remember?" Rachel sarcastically remarked, making Scarlett laugh and relax into her.

"Have you heard of MDLG before? Because I think that you'd love it," Rachel said as she began to rock Scarlett on her lap and wrap her arms around Scarlett's waist.

"Maybe," Scarlett said, giggling and

burying her face into Rachel's neck. Rachel held Scarlett's head in place as she rocked her, enjoying feeling her relax and melt onto her lap.

"I thought so," Rachel replied, smiling to herself. Scarlett began looking at Rachel's neck, the long lines, and bits of hair that had fallen, causing Rachel to reach up and pull it out, letting it flow down her back and tickle Scarlett, making her laugh.

"Such a sweetheart. You're not so big and tough, are you, little one?" Rachel said, smirking as she saw the mischievous look in Scarlett's eyes and the cheeky smile on her face.

"No, I just always had to be," Scarlett replied, shaking her head and shrugging her shoulders.

"But not anymore," Rachel quickly added, taking out a paci from her top drawer and pushing it into Scarlett's mouth, taking her by surprise.

"You leave that in little miss," Rachel said, pushing it back in as Scarlett took it out.

"You're going to be a good girl for me," Rachel warned, causing Scarlett to place her hand on Rachel's breast, taking her by surprise.

"Cheeky girl," Rachel said, smiling and letting Scarlett gently grab at her. Rachel leaned back against her chair and let Scarlett begin to explore her body. She loved seeing Scarlett get lost in her and imagined taking her home and babying her for the night, just as Scarlett sighed and resting her head against Rachel's chest.

"You're so lovely," Rachel sighed, stroking Scarlett's back and almost putting her to sleep.

"I should probs see another shrink now, right?" Scarlett said as the alarm went off on their session. Rachel had rocked Scarlett on her lap their whole time together, enjoying Scarlett's little outburst of tears, as she was loved and nurtured.

"Well, that's something that I wanted to talk to you about. How would you feel having a play session here, so still coming here, and I can just sign you off as coming, but we play instead? If you want to actually commit to therapy, then yes, you should see another therapist," Rachel said. Scarlett just gave her a one-sided smile.

"I kinda don't want to. I don't think I need therapy. I think I might need this," Scarlett softly replied, looking at Rachel timidly, not wanting to be rejected. Rachel stood up and walked to where Scarlett was standing. She reached out and ran her fingers through Scarlett's hair, holding her head back and making her look up at her. The look of lust and passion in Rachel's eyes was reflected in Scarlett's, and the two of them stood as time seemed to stop around them.

"Yeah, I'd love that," Scarlett replied, breaking their eye contact and picking up her wallet and walking out the door.

Chapter 7

"Tell me some of the things that you'd like to try," Rachel said down the phone Saturday night. Emily and Scott had gone out to a restaurant, meaning that Scarlett had the whole house to herself for a few hours.

"I don't know, I like cuddling with you," Scarlett said, letting her fingers play with her panty covered pussy.

"Tell me what you are wearing," Rachel sensually instructed, making Scarlett giggle.

"Do you like it when I tell you what to do?" Rachel asked, making a mental note.

"Yeah," Scarlett replied, feeling her wetness between her pussy lips.

"Yes, Mommy," Rachel corrected, smirking as she heard Scarlett's breathing come in short sharp pants.

"Yes, Mommy," Scarlett repeated, rubbing her clit. She closed her eyes and arched her back, aching for release.

"Mommy wants you to stop playing with yourself now," Rachel sternly said, causing Scarlett's eyes to open as she reluctantly took her hand away.

"Good girl," Rachel said, hearing her soft whine in frustration.

"Tell me what other things you like. I already know you like a paci, do you like coloring and making things?" Rachel asked. Scarlett bit her bottom lip as she thought about the different things that she had only ever thought of doing and smiled.

"I guess. I haven't ever really explored it too much before, I kinda just like calling you Mommy. I don't know what else I like," Scarlett honestly replied, making Rachel's heart swell.

"Okay, well would you be happy to let Mommy take the lead tomorrow, and you can say you want it to stop whenever you want," Rachel said, Scarlett, giving her puppy dog eyes and nodding, even though they were on the phone.

"Alright, see you tomorrow," Scarlett replied, hanging up the phone and going back to touching herself. She couldn't believe how her life was turning out. Sure, the start was a bit hit and miss, but now she had the type of Mommy she had dreamed of, was almost ready to move into her own place, and had a killer wardrobe.

Not so bad, for a bad kid, she thought as she pleasured herself, not hearing the front door open. Scarlett teased her clit, running her fingers down the sides and into her pussy, closing her eyes and rolling her head back as she arched her back, wanting a deeper penetration.

"That's not what good little girls should be doing," Emily said, leaning against the wall and making Scarlett gasp and freeze.

"I, um," Scarlett stammered as Scott peered around the door, seeing his friend in just her t-shirt and panties.

"Emily, I'm really sorry," Scarlett apologetically said. It had been clear from the first day that she was there that Emily ruled this household, and even though she did it nicely, there was no question in Scarlett's mind, Emily was the boss.

"Scarlett, do you want to play with us?" Emily said, walking into the room and sitting on the end of the bed, gently taking Scarlett's hand from her pussy. Scarlett couldn't deny that Emily was gorgeous, but she didn't really know how it would make her friendship turn out with Scott.

"Oh, don't worry about him, I know you don't want his cock," Emily said, making both Scott and Scarlett laugh.

"Yeah, okay," Scarlett excitedly but nervously said, smiling and wondering what would happen next.

"Good," Emily replied, kicking off her shoes and smirking at Scarlett.

"Scott, sit on the floor. You're going to find this torturous, and I am going to love every moment of your pain," Emily said, her voice changing and making Scarlett frown.

"Take off the rest of these clothes," Emily

said, turning to face Scarlett. Scarlett felt the dynamic shift as Emily went from the authoritarian but soft and gentle woman she had come to know, into somebody harsher, with a cruel look in their eye. She tried to brush it off, telling herself that she could leave at any time she wanted.

"Kneel on the bed for me," Emily said, interrupting Scarlett's thoughts, her body moving to Emily's request.

"Like this," Emily sternly said, grabbing Scarlett's arms and putting them behind her head and pushing her thighs apart.

"I'd be lying if I said that I hadn't thought about you in that position for days," Emily said almost to herself, reaching out and cupping Scarlett's pussy, causing her to gasp and pull away from her.

"Where do you think you are going?" Emily said, gently slapping Scarlett's ass and putting her back into the position. Scarlett bit her lip, feeling herself become aroused by

Emily's aggressive manner, moaning as Emily felt how wet Scarlett was, smiling as she did so.

"I knew that you'd like this," Emily whispered into Scarlett's ear, only leaving her pussy to begin to rub her breasts. Scarlett thought about Rachel. Her soft embrace, the way she held onto Scarlett as she had cried. Her sweet but subtle smelling perfume that seemed to calm Scarlett's tortured heart, just as she felt Emily's leather flogger on her ass.

"Ouch," Scarlett involuntarily said, snapping out of her daydream and looking at Emily's face.

"I said, turn around," Emily commanded, making Scarlett laugh.

"Yeah, um, I'm out. I don't want to do this anymore," Scarlett said, getting up and beginning to put her clothes on, clearly surprising Emily.

"Oh, okay then," Emily said, snapping her fingers at Scott, who followed her out of the room. Scarlett pulled on her house clothes and lay on the bed, taking her phone out and wishing that Rachel had messaged her.

She's just doing her job. It's not personal. She doesn't want you, Scarlett told herself, trying to stop any transference she was feeling from taking over her mind.

But I mean, we do play a little. Like, calling her Mommy is amazing, Scarlett continued thinking, wondering if she was reading more into it than Rachel was intending, or if she was reading it correctly.

"Knock, knock," Scarlett timidly said as she saw the door to Rachel's office slightly opened the following day.

"Hi, sweetie, come in," Rachel said, jumping up from her black office chair and standing up, just as Scarlett walked into the room.

"Um, what's all this?" Scarlett said as she looked around at the play gym on the floor. Rachel smiled and sat back down, placing her hands in her pockets.

"Well, I thought that maybe you would want to try going a little further. I know that you liked cuddling, I wondered if you'd like this as well," Rachel explained, making Scarlett laugh.

"I don't really feel in that sort of headspace today. The people that I'm staying with, well, we tried to have sex last night, and it was just, really bad," Scarlett replied, Rachel, raising an eyebrow, her curiosity piqued. Although she knew that Scarlett wasn't hers, Rachel was taken aback and had to check herself before she continued to speak.

"Why was it bad?" She asked. Scarlett sighed and sat back on the couch, looking at the play gym mat with its cartoon animals and colorful shapes.

"She just got really rough, and like, I wasn't down for it," Scarlett said, folding her arms across her chest.

"Did it remind you of something?" Rachel said, coping a glare from Scarlett.

"I just mean, I can't imagine prison was easy for you. Could it have been that the rough sex that she was wanting made you remember your time in prison?" Rachel backtracked, happy when Scarlett's expression softened.

"Maybe," she answered, making Rachel smile as she watched Scarlett look at the gym.

"Do you want to cuddle again?" Rachel asked, seeing Scarlett pulled her arms closer around herself. Scarlett subtly nodded, surprised that Rachel could bring her into her little space with almost no effort at all.

"Come here then," Rachel said, turning her chair and holding out her hand to Scarlett. Scarlett sat on Rachel's lap, enjoying how it felt to have her gentle touch as Rachel rubbed her back. Scarlett dropped her head, closed her eyes, and relaxed into Rachel's embrace.

"I wish you were my Mommy," Scarlett involuntarily said, gasping and looking up when she realized what she had said.

"Sorry, I," Scarlett said, trying to get up,

surprised when Rachel held her in place.

"You don't have to run away from me," Rachel replied, smiling, happy that Scarlett had just confessed her deepest desires.

"I wish you were my baby girl, too," Rachel confessed, taking Scarlett by surprise. They stayed like that, Rachel holding onto Scarlett for the longest of times before Scarlett began to wiggle on Rachel's lap.

"Do you want to hop down, little one?" Rachel asked, Scarlett, giving her her big puppy dog eyes and smirking.

"I wanna play with that," Scarlett replied, pointing at the play gym. Rachel took her arms away from around Scarlett's waist and let her hop onto the floor, kicking her shoes off as she did so.

"Can I come down and play with you?" Rachel asked, Scarlett, nodding her head as she hit the toys which hung overhead.

"I didn't know they came in such big sizes," Scarlett happily said, touching all the hanging toys. Rachel couldn't help but fall for Scarlett's happy face and playful personality, deciding that it was best that Scarlett see another therapist.

"Baby," Rachel said, getting Scarlett's attention.

"Would you be interested in getting to know me a little bit more, maybe, have dinner with me?" Rachel asked. In her time as a therapist, she had never fallen for a client as hard as she had Scarlett, and the thought of not having Scarlett as her own filled her with disappointment. Scarlett thought for a moment, surprised that Rachel was trying to move their dynamic forward. She looked at Rachel, wondering how to respond correctly.

"You can say no if you want, that's absolutely no problem, and we can keep doing what we are doing here. If that makes you more comfortable?" Rachel began to say, not wanting to push Scarlett too far out of her comfort zone.

"No, I would really like that," Scarlett

suddenly replied, not wanting Rachel to take the offer away and giving Rachel one more cheeky smile before going back to play with the play gym.

Chapter 8

Rachel looked at the clock on her wall and smiled, knowing she still had 30minutes with Scarlett before their session ended.

"What are you playing with, baby?" Rachel asked, looking at Scarlett and brushing the hair out of her eyes.

"The lion," Scarlett replied, surprising Rachel when she put it down and looked at her seductively.

"But I want to play with something else," Scarlett smirked, looking at Rachel and casually putting her hand on her thigh. Rachel raised an eyebrow. It wasn't the first time that a client had wanted to have sex with her or vice versa, but it was the first time that a client had instigated sex.

"Are you being a cheeky girl?" Rachel said, laughing at Scarlett's innocent face.

"Maybe," Scarlett softly said, giggling as Rachel, flipping her onto her back and knelt over her face.

"Do you do this with your other clients?" Scarlett asked. Rachel just shook her head before slowly bringing her lips down to touch Scarlett's, enjoying the gasp of surprise that she elicited.

"Is this what you wanted?" Rachel asked, allowing her body to fall onto Scarlett's gently. Scarlett moaned as she kissed Rachel back, feeling the older woman's hands gently touching her body and fanning the fire that had been building for weeks.

"Yes," Scarlett desperately moaned as she arched her back and rolled her head back, feeling Rachel kiss her again, more passionately this time. Scarlett loved that she could feel Rachel getting lost in their kiss, feeling her hands softly grabbing at her breasts and thighs and taking her to a place of safety and arousal.

"Does that feel good, baby?" Rachel seductively whispered into Scarlett's ear as she slowly felt over Scarlett's clothes.

"You are making Mommy horny sweet

girl," Rachel said as she stopped herself, wanting to pull off Scarlett's shirt.

"You can," Scarlett replied, helping Rachel do so.

"Honey, take those hands and put them behind your head for Mommy," Rachel said, climbing on top of Scarlett.

"You'll be a good girl for me, won't you?" Rachel moaned as she began to slowly take off Scarlett's shirt and bra, kissing along her collar bone.

"I don't want to go any further," Scarlett said, gently pushing Rachel away, worried that she would be angry just like Emily.

"That's alright, honey," Rachel replied, pulling Scarlett into her arms and holding her tightly. Scarlett was surprised at how okay Rachel was with ending their play. It wasn't conditional like with Esther or Ross, and she wasn't super angry about it like Emily had been.

"I guess this isn't what you're meant to do with your clients, huh?" Scarlett said, turning in

Rachel's arms and looking up at her.

"No, and if I'm being honest, I could be in a lot of trouble for this. But you're worth it," Rachel laughed, before becoming serious.

"But I still think it's a good idea for you to go to another therapist because there are some things that you need to sort through, but I just want a different role with you, and from the looks of things, you want that too," she added beaming down at Scarlett.

"Yeah, I think that might be a good idea. I also think that I'd like to take you out somewhere nice and get to know you better. I guess this whole thing isn't really starting the way it should. Can I change the tempo a little bit?" Scarlett asked, Rachel, tilting her head to the side and curiously looking at Scarlett. Scarlett was surprised that she felt like she had so much control in the dynamic that she was creating with Rachel.

Usually, I would just let her do whatever she wants. I just let anyone do whatever they wanted. It feels good to have some control and for that to be respected, Scarlett said to herself

"Yeah sure, tell me about what you want," Rachel said, smiling as she saw Scarlett feeling empowered.

"Okay. I want to take you somewhere nice and just talk like adults. I don't want any teasing or suggestive stuff. Then I want to see if we click outside this dynamic of doctor and patient and then maybe start something with you. I want to backtrack a little bit. I hope that's alright?" Scarlett said, holding her breath and hoping that by setting her boundaries, she wasn't going to lose Rachel.

"That sounds like a very wise decision," Rachel replied, nodding her head and putting all of Scarlett's fears aside.

"Can I just say one more thing before I go?" Scarlett added, getting up and walking to the door. Rachel could see the cheeky look in Scarlett's eye and knew that whatever was coming next would be good.

"Sure," Rachel said, trying to hide her excitement.

"Your tits are amazing," Scarlett said, reaching out and playing with them, making Rachel laugh. She allowed Scarlett to have her fun before taking her hands in hers and holding them behind her back.

"That's enough now, you've had your fun, now let's try to keep to those rules you just set," Rachel said, opening the door and walking Scarlett out of the office, her cheeky smile refusing to leave her face.

Scarlett walked down the street feeling light and full of happiness, turned the corner, and saw Emily and Scott arrive home, immediately feeling the change in her mood. Things had been awkward between the three of them, and all Scarlett knew was that she needed to get out of that house before things got any worse. She grimaced at them, walked into the house, and all but ran to her room, sitting on the bed and sighing, happy that she had gotten passed them without having to talk.

"Hi," Scarlett said to Scott when he peered around the corner.

So much for my lucky escape, Scarlett thought to herself. Scott had taken Emily's side in this silent argument, but Scarlett didn't blame him.

We aren't the same people we were all those years ago, and I mean, I wouldn't want to risk losing all this either, she said to herself, looking at how Scott was clearly uncomfortable.

"Hey, so, I am just going to come straight out and say it, Emily wants you out of the house," Scott said. Scarlett could tell it was as awkward for him as it was for her, and it made her smile.

"Yeah, don't worry, I actually got paid today, so I'll be able to get out of your hair in a few weeks," Scarlett replied, a questioning look on her face when Scott pulled a face.

"Yeah, um, she kinda means, like, right

now," Scott said, making Scarlett's eye go wide. She sighed, fell back on the bed, and felt her eyes begin to well up.

"Is this because I didn't want to fuck her the way she wanted? This is such bullshit," Scarlett replied, wiping her tears and getting up, going to her cupboard and taking a bag out. Scott just nervously walked out of the room and shut the door on Scarlett as she began to throw clothes into her bag as she cried.

Typical, everything has to go right, and then everything just goes wrong. I should have just let her fuck me, Scarlett said to herself, knowing that she had nowhere else to go. She sat on her bed, trying to push her tears back down before she left the house.

I can't let her see me cry. I'm not going to give that bitch the satisfaction, she thought, wiping her tears and taking some deep breaths. She got up, walked to the cupboard, and packed a couple of tins of food and packets of cookies before giving Emily the finger as she headed to the door.

I can't let myself be homeless. They'll find a way to put me back in there, I just know it, Scarlett thought, opening the door and looking back at Scott. She knew that this would be the last time that she spoke or saw him again, and she wanted to remember. She wanted to remember him as the boy she had grown up with, not the man who let his woman kick her out of the house because she had turned her down sexually.

I guess it's true. You don't finish with everyone you start with, Scarlett thought as she continued to look at Scott, who was looking apologetically at Scarlett as she slammed the front door behind herself.

"What a fucking bitch," Scarlett said out loud as she began to walk up the street. She didn't know where she was going, all she knew was that she needed somewhere safe to sleep for the night.

Oh fuck, Rachel, Scarlett suddenly

thought, remembering that she had organized to see Rachel that evening. Scarlett made her way to a sidewalk bench and sat down. She knew that she was in the middle of a panic attack by the way her palms became sweaty, and she wanted to run away from everything.

I could, turn my phone off, hitch a ride out of town and change my name and start a new life somewhere else, Scarlett thought, smiling when she knew that she wasn't actually going to do that. Starting over had been significantly harder in practice than it was in theory, and the task of re-starting over made her uneasy.

Or I could be a grown-up, message Rachel what is going on. If I'm really lucky she'll let me stay with her and if not then that's also cool, but either way, we aren't going to go anywhere tonight, Scarlett decided, taking out her phone and dialing Rachel's number.

"Hi baby," Rachel answered, surprised that Scarlett was ringing her when only a few hours ago they had spoken.

"Hey, so, I'm not trying to get out of hanging out with you, and I'm not asking you for any favors. But the people that I was staying with kicked me out, and I have nowhere else to go so I can't hang out with you tonight because I need to find a place to stay for a while," Scarlett explained, smiling to herself that she felt like she could handle this situation.

"Oh, sweetie," Rachel said, wondering if it would be too much to offer Scarlett to stay with her.

She wanted to take things slowly, you asking her to stay isn't slowly! Rachel thought to herself, biting her lip as she thought.

"I have an idea, and you can turn me down without me losing any interest in you, alright. Do you want to stay with me for a few nights? We can keep things going slowly, but I don't want you on the streets or in a shelter," Rachel replied, hoping that Scarlett would take her up on the offer.

"I don't want to sleep in the same bed as you, and I really don't want anything to happen. Getting out of prison has proven to be harder than being in there. At least in there, everything was predictable, and I knew what the deal was, out here, everything is so unstructured and unpredictable," Scarlett said, starting to cry. She felt so pathetic.

"Oh, baby. Don't cry. It'll be okay. Mommy is going to make everything alright. Where are you, send me your location, I'm coming to get you, alright?" Rachel said, getting off the couch and grabbing her keys.

"Okay. Thanks, Rachel," Scarlett replied between sobs, hanging up and sending Rachel her location. Scarlett put her phone back into her pocket, placed her bag between her feet, closed her eyes, and waited for Rachel to pick her up.

"I feel really embarrassed, thanks for this," Scarlett said, feeling like the damsel in distress that was just saved by her princess charming as she sat in Rachel's car, playing with the hem of her shorts. Scarlett felt like one of the adult videos she had watched where some young, helpless girl gets picked up by a hot mature woman and then fucked the moment she gets taken to the woman's house.

"It's no trouble, I just hope that you aren't put off by my house, it's pretty basic, like nice, but nothing fancy," Rachel said, surprising herself that she felt insecure about her place.

"I just got out of jail, so like, as long as there's no one jumping me in the shower, it'll be amazing," Scarlett replied, realizing that it was the first time that she had acknowledged the truth of what had happened to her in the last week of her sentence.

"Did you just?" Rachel asked, stopping when she saw Scarlett's smirking face.

"Yeah, I did. Progress," Scarlett replied, laughing and reaching out to hold Rachel's hand.

"You know, I think it's really nice that you let me set the pace for everything. I kinda didn't think that that was something that I was allowed to do. I hope that you don't think that I am bratty or something because of it," Scarlett said, noticing the knot in her stomach, worried that she wouldn't be what Rachel wanted and that Rachel would kick her out as well.

"No, I don't think that at all. What I think is that you are trying to protect yourself, which I think is very wise. But in time, you'll learn that you can trust me, even though I bent the rules so that we could have this," Rachel replied, placing her hand on Scarlett's thigh and gently squeezing. Scarlett looked out the window and closed her eyes as she felt herself slowly relax.

This is nice. It might not have been how I thought it would go, but the plan is still working. I'm safe, I think, and Rachel is gorgeous, Scarlett thought, smiling as she felt the warm afternoon sun on her face.

"We're here," Rachel announced, pulling into the driveway. The cottage style house made Scarlett smile.

This looks like the types of homes in those fancy country magazines, Scarlett thought as she looked out the window at the white wooden cottage with the green garden and cobblestone garden path. The lavender on the front porch and the red and pink roses on the window sill made Rachel's house look like a postcard.

"You were worried about this?! This is cute," Scarlett said, making Rachel smile. She was happy that Scarlett liked her place.

"Come on, let's get you inside," Rachel said, unbuckling Scarlett's seat belt before heading toward the front door.

"What?" Rachel said, turning around to see that Scarlett was standing in front of the car.

"Don't you think it's a bit weird?" Scarlett asked, kicking the stones with her shoe. Rachel smiled and thought for a moment, unsure of what to say.

"Maybe if you didn't want me, it would be weird. But I've only ever given you what you needed and wanted. Is it so bad that I want to look after you?" Rachel questioned, placing her hands on either side of Scarlett's face and tucking her hair behind her ears.

"I guess not," Scarlett replied, stretching out her arms and holding onto Rachel, relaxing into her just as Rachel released her.

"Alright then," Rachel stated, taking Scarlett's hand and walking her through the front door. Rachel kicked her shoes off by the door and continued to walk Scarlett through the house and into the front room bedroom.

"You can put your things down here if you like," Rachel said, turning to look at Scarlett, who was smirking at the stuffie on the bed.

"I thought you might like it," Rachel said, her fake innocence making Scarlett shake her head.

"You're trouble," Scarlett replied, dropping her bag and sighing. She sat on the bed and thought about how she felt like a passenger to her life, that somehow, someone else was always driving the car, and she was just there reacting to their control.

"I think I need a shower. I'm really tired," Scarlett said, looking up at Rachel, who smiled down at her.

"Do you want me to run it for you?" Rachel asked, feeling herself slip into Mommy space. Scarlett just shrugged her shoulders and looked at the ground.

"What is it, baby?" Rachel asked, sitting down on the bed next to Scarlett. Scarlett shook her head, unable to decide what it was that was hurting her heart with such intensity.

"I don't know. I just feel sad," Scarlett said, beginning to cry. Rachel reached out and took Scarlett into her arms, slowly rocking her and holding her close.

"I know that everything seems a bit too much right now, baby. But it'll feel better soon," Rachel affectionately said, waiting until Scarlett's tears stopped flowing before she let her go.

"I think maybe I just want to shower by myself," Scarlett said, getting up and kicking her shoes off. She looked at Rachel, almost asking for permission as she put her hands in her pockets and deeply inhaled.

"Whatever you need, sweetie," Rachel affectionately said, getting up and kissing her forehead before walking out the door.
Scarlett walked into the bathroom and shut the door behind her, sighing.

This is my life now, Scarlett thought to herself, looking around the bathroom, smiling a smile of relief. She thought back to the times where she would shower with her back to the wall, worried that somebody was going to try and hurt her.

No one can hurt you now, she said to herself. She turned the water on, stripped her clothes off, and waited for the water to become warm.

I can't let myself care. I just can't fucking care about them, she thought, standing under the water and feeling the guilt of finally looking after herself. She thought back to her family, always having to scrape together money for food, clothes, she remembered how cold her hands and feet used to be, the cold seeping into her bones, and how she would sleep with her knees to her chest to try and stay warm. She felt guilty for leaving them behind, feeling like an imposter in Rachel's house.

I should have gone back to them. I shouldn't have stayed with Scott, Scarlett thought. She remembered how whenever she had tried to ring them while she was away, they'd never ask how she was, only ever telling her drama that had happened and how drunk this person had gotten or that someone at a party had stolen their cigarettes.

I guess that's not the life I wanted either, Scarlett said to herself. Scarlett felt embarrassed about where she had come from, trying to figure out how she was going to explain who she really was to Rachel.

What will she think when she finds out? Yeah, she knows that I must have had a rough start by the fact that I ended up in jail, but what if I'm too trashy for her, Scarlett thought, washing her body and seeming to gasp under the water as her nervous system tried to regulate itself. She hadn't noticed that she was sitting on the shower floor until she heard the knock come from the door.

"Scarlett?" Rachel questioned, opening the door and cautiously peering in.

"Are you alright?" She asked, seeing Scarlett slowly standing up. Scarlett wrapped a towel around herself and ran her fingers through her hair.

"Yeah, sorry," Scarlett replied, making Rachel smile, relief in her eyes.

"You don't have to be sorry. I was just worried, you've been in here a really long time," Rachel explained, opening up her arms to Scarlett, who snuggled in close to her.

"Come on, do you want me to look after you tonight?" Rachel asked, walking Scarlett into her bedroom.

"Yes, please," Scarlett softly said, feeling herself slipping into her little space. That was all she wanted, somebody to take care of her, to make sure that she had everything she needed and to do everything for her.

Wow, I'm really clingy and needy, Scarlett thought, smirking to herself. After so many years of being alone, having someone who wanted to look after her made her head spin.

"Alright, little one," Rachel said, putting up her hair and taking a few things down from her cupboard shelf. Scarlett knew she was feeling little, as she sucked her thumb, happy when Rachel took her thumb out of her mouth and replaced it with a paci.

"Mommy's sweet girl," Rachel cooed, taking the towel away and sliding a diaper under Scarlett.

"Let's get you all ready for bed. I can't have my pretty girl falling asleep without a diaper," Rachel said, powdering Scarlett, who reached for her.

"Hold on, sweetie, Mommy is almost done," Rachel smiled, she loved how needy and clingy Scarlett was and fastened the tabs tightly around her waist. She reached for a light blue onesie and quickly dressed Scarlett, before taking her back to the bathroom and drying her hair.

"There, all ready for Mommy cuddles," Rachel said as she ran her fingers through Scarlett's hair and felt her head fall into her chest.

"This is nice," Scarlett softly said, holding onto Rachel like she held all the answers to every question Scarlett could ever have.

Chapter 9

Scarlett stayed in Rachel's arms all night, having panic attack after panic attack until she finally fell asleep in the early hours of the morning.

"My sweet girl," Rachel whispered, kissing Scarlett's forehead after holding her for hours, her tears soaking the top of Rachel's shirt as Scarlett stirred in her sleep, exhausted after feeling her heart slowly begin to heal. Rachel gave Scarlett everything she was looking for, but it came at a cost. The cost was honesty. Scarlett couldn't pretend everything was fine with Rachel, and as Rachel had soothed her broken, fragile heart through the night, Scarlett knew that Rachel was the woman she had always wished to find.

"Good morning, pretty girl," Rachel said as Scarlett blinked her eyes open. Scarlett's tears had sealed her eyes shut and rubbing them, Rachel smile and led her to the bathroom.

"Let Mommy wash your face," Rachel said, kissing Scarlett's cheeks as she took a washcloth and dampened it with warm water. Gently rubbing Scarlett's eyes clean, she opened them, their sparkly blue hue seducing Rachel without Scarlett even having to try.

"I have to go to work today," Scarlett said, biting her lip and looking down at her onesie and diaper.

"I guess you can't go like that, can you?" Rachel laughed, smiling, and nodding her head as Scarlett began to undress, looking at Rachel for permission.

"Do you want breakfast before you go?" Rachel asked, trying to hide the fact that Scarlett's naked body drove her wild as Scarlett walked back to the bedroom and started getting dressed for work.

"No, I'll get something there," Scarlett called, putting on her lingerie and turning to face Rachel.

"Don't look at me like that," Scarlett

giggled, Rachel, crossing her arms over her chest and leaning against the wall.

"I can look at you any way I want to," she seductively said, making Scarlett roll her eyes.

"Not if I don't let you," Scarlett replied, her cheeky smile encouraging Rachel.   "Well, that is true, but would you really want Mommy to not be interested in you?" She questioned, walking forward and wrapping her arms around Scarlett, and throwing her down on the bed.

"Mommy," Scarlett giggled, pushing her off and sitting next to her.

"I can't right now," Scarlett added, the seriousness in her tone telling Rachel all she needed to know.

"Alright, baby," Rachel said, reaching out to tuck a strand of hair behind Scarlett's ear.

"I've got to go," Scarlett said, standing up and pulling her jeans on.

"Do you need a lift?" Rachel asked, wishing that she was able to look after Scarlett more than she was letting her.

"No, it's cool, thanks, though, maybe tomorrow? I've got a late shift, and I kinda hate working them because they feel more dangerous than working a day shift," Scarlett explained, grabbing her bag and standing by the front door as she buttoned up her shirt.

"Well, that's because they are, so yes, I'll drive you to work tomorrow," Rachel said, feeling Scarlett suddenly wrap her arms around her neck and hold her tightly.

"See you later," Scarlett said, kissing Rachel before she left.

Scarlett walked down the street and towards her work, feeling all loved up from the night before.

Oh, I could have stayed in her arms forever, she thought, as she remembered Rachel's gentle stroking on her back and the way she fit perfectly against her body. Scarlett pushed the doors of the diner open and smiled as she walked toward the back.

Life is good, even if I have these fucking

dishes to do, Scarlett said to herself, signing and rolling up her sleeves, beginning her shift. Little did she know, as she had passed through the diner, she had caught the attention of the warden, who was having brunch with one of the guards.

"Was that?" The guard said, Esther's eyes sparkling with delight.

"Yes, it was," she replied. This wasn't the usual place the warden came when she wanted to have vanilla pancakes, but her usual joint was closed for renovations.

"It's always so strange seeing them in the real world," the guard said, smirking when Esther got up and cracked her neck.

"Where are you going?" The guard asked, already knowing the answer. Esther just turned and looked at them, winking and turning back to begin to walk into the back of the diner.

"Hi," Esther said, Scarlett, turning around, her mouth gaped open as though she had just seen a ghost.

"What are you doing here?" Scarlett asked. Her words surprised not only the warden but herself as well.

Careful, Scarlett said to herself, unsure of her level of safety.

"I saw you come in, and I thought I'd say hi," Esther replied, putting her hands in her pockets.

"I see you've kept yourself out of trouble," Esther added, coming up behind Scarlett and wrapping her arms around her.

"You can't do that to me anymore," Scarlett said, slipping out from her gasp and wiping her wet hands on her apron.

"You weren't complaining last time," Esther said, clearly offended.

"Last time, I had no choice. It wasn't exactly an even power dynamic," Scarlett replied, annoyed that she could feel Esther getting to her.

"You should leave," Scarlett said, putting her hands on her hips. Esther looked at her, standing in front of her, being empowered, and didn't like it.

"Do you think you're better than me now or something? We aren't on the same level. You'll always be a shit kicker, having to work shitty jobs because you're trash. You came from trash, and you'll die trash. You were only ever good for a fun time. That's all you'll ever be good for," Esther said before leaving Scarlett, just as the tears she was trying so desperately to keep from falling, escaped her eyes.

Don't listen to her, don't listen to her, Scarlett told herself, feeling herself have another panic attack. She took off her apron and grabbed her bag, rushing out of the diner as her boss yelled at her for leaving, but she couldn't hear the words he was shouting as she ran out onto the street. Scarlett could feel her heart beating in her throat. She felt like she was going to be sick as she pushed past the people and felt her head spin. She knew that she needed to get home. She knew what she wanted.

"Mommy!" Scarlett frantically yelled as she opened the door to Rachel's house and dropped her bag and then herself to the floor.

"Baby?" Rachel questioned, the concern and compassion in her voice bring Scarlett to tears.

"I'm sorry, I'm so sorry," Scarlett sobbed over and over. Rachel had questions, hundreds of them, but she knew that Scarlett wouldn't be able to answer any of them until she had calmed down.

"Can Mommy look after you?" Rachel softly asked, holding Scarlett's tear-stained face in her hands. Scarlett nodded, feeling more pathetic than she had ever felt in her life.

"It's alright, little bunny, Mommy knows what you need. You're a good girl, come here," Rachel said, picking Scarlett up and taking to the couch. Rachel set her up with blankets and her paci, smiling when she sat next to Scarlett

"Do you want anything else?" Rachel asked, enjoying how Scarlett pawed at her breasts.

"Yes, Mommy," Scarlett timidly replied, allowing Rachel to position her and letting her suckle.

"Don't try to tell Mommy yet," Rachel said, seeing Scarlett begin to try and talk. Rachel rocked Scarlett until her sobs ended, and her eyes closed, body relaxed, and began to feel heavy.

"Mommy's going to look after you, sweetie. I think you should give work a miss for now," Rachel said, smiling down at Scarlett, who cuddled into her.

"I saw her," Scarlett softly said, moving so that her face was in the crock of Rachel's neck. Rachel stroked Scarlett's back and held her tight on her lap.

"Who did you see, baby?" Rachel asked, leaning back against the couch, enjoying how it felt to hold Scarlett.

"Esther, the warden from jail," Scarlett whispered. Rachel could feel herself becoming defensive and protective, already hating where this conversation was going to lead.

"Do you want to tell Mommy what happened?" Rachel asked. Scarlett nodded her head and looked up into Rachel's loving eyes.

"I started my shift, and she was just there. Like she just appeared out of nowhere," Scarlett started to explain. She liked that Rachel didn't ask any questions; she just held her and listened, making her feel safe and loved.

"And then she started to say all this stuff about how I'm nothing and that I'm only good for sex," Scarlett said, feeling her tears begin to fall onto her cheeks.

"Oh baby," Rachel replied, kissing her tears away and rocking her.

"I'm happy you came home to Mommy," Rachel said. She knew that she would be able to support Scarlett for a few months while she found a new job, she sure wasn't about to let her go back to the diner now that the warden knew where she worked.

"I know it's the middle of the day, but I think you need Mommy to look after you," Rachel said, beginning to take Scarlett's uniform off.

"You aren't going to need that anymore. I don't want you going back to the diner, baby. Do you understand me?" Rachel said, her stern words making Scarlett's eyes go wide.

"You don't have to be scared of Mommy. You just have to follow Mommy's rules, alright?" Rachel said, standing Scarlett up and waiting for her to nod her head before taking her into the bedroom.

"I'm happy it's the weekend," Rachel said, diapering Scarlett and putting her into a pink fluffy diaper cover and a white shirt, a pink bow in her hair, and her pink paci in her mouth.

"You're going to stay Mommy's baby for the rest of the weekend," Rachel lovingly said, as Scarlett touched the front of her diaper.

"Yes, that does mean that you'll wet your diaper for Mommy," Rachel added, reading

Scarlett's mind.

Chapter 10

"Mommy," Scarlett whined. It had been three hours since she had been put in her diaper, and Rachel had been waiting.

"Well, if you just use your diaper like a good girl, Mommy will change you," Rachel replied. She had put a movie on for Scarlett, who was cuddling in next to her and would bury her face in her lap at every scary part.

"We could go to the art gallery and have a picnic if you'd like, sweetie?" Rachel asked, just as the movie ended. Scarlett's eyes went wide, making Rachel laugh.

"No, I would put you in something a little more discrete," Rachel laughed. She ran her fingers through Scarlett's hair and wondered what it would take for Scarlett to wet her diaper.

"I don't wanna," Scarlett whined, shaking her head from side to side and pouting. Rachel liked seeing this side of Scarlett. It was one thing to have a good girl. It was another to have a girl who was confident that the relationship would be fine if it got tested.

"You don't want to be a bad girl for Mommy," Rachel whispered, sending shivers down Scarlett's arms.

"Exactly, good idea," Rachel added, seeing Scarlett's eyes go wide with innocence once more and her diaper become wet.

"Let's get you cleaned up and ready to go out," Rachel said, taking Scarlett's hand and leading her to the bedroom. Rachel put out a changing mat and snapped her fingers and pointing to the floor.

"Lay down for Mommy," Rachel commanded, happy when Scarlett followed her orders. Rachel looked through her cupboard. Scarlett's clothes hung next to hers, the collection of adult baby outfits, just discrete enough that no one would be the wiser unless they were someway kink inclined.

"Those, Mommy," Scarlett said, pointing

to the pair of baggy overalls.

"Please, Mommy," Rachel corrected, enjoying the blushing checks she gave Scarlett.

"Oh, you don't have to be embarrassed little baby. Mommy's not mad. But I'd be a bad Mommy if I didn't teach you to use your manners," Rachel said, coming to where Scarlett was laying down and kissing Scarlett's forehead.

"Please, Mommy," Scarlett softly replied, smiling when Rachel began to change her diaper.

"Mommy, I can't!" She was suddenly exclaiming and wriggling on the mat when she saw Rachel take down a diaper.

"Oh yes, you can, and you will," Rachel replied, playfully spanking Scarlett's thighs.

"Lift up for Mommy," Rachel said, seeing Scarlett obey her.

"Good girl. Mommy was going to put this big vibrator into your little pussy and make you have that inside of you while we were out if you hadn't stopped being naughty. Lucky for you, you remembered your manners," Rachel said, beginning to lube a small buttplug.

"But Mommy, you said I was good," Scarlett said, her eyes going wide. Rachel leaned forward and kissed Scarlett on the nose, enjoying how her heavy breasts pushed into Scarlett's tummy.

"I know you were good. This isn't a punishment, baby. This is something to enjoy," Rachel replied, pushing the tip into Scarlett and getting turned on by her soft moans as the plug filled her. Rubbing her fingers over the clear crystal at the end and pushing it into Scarlett, Rachel went back to diapering her. Scarlett felt it immediately, the sensation of the plug, making her clit tingle, and she reached down to touch herself, making Rachel smirk.

"No baby, we don't touch ourselves there," Rachel said, taking Scarlett's hands away as she arched her back, wanting her clit to stop throbbing.

"Oh, is somebody a little bit horny now?" Rachel said, enjoying watching Scarlett's clit harden. Scarlett nodded her head and reached for Rachel, warming her heart.

"Not right now, baby. But if you are a good girl for me, on the way home, I'll give you a special reward," Rachel explained, making Scarlett bring her arms down to her chest and waited for Rachel to finish diapering her. Next, Rachel pulled on the overalls, some pink socks, and a pink t-shirt along with yellow Converse sneakers and put Scarlett's hair in a messy ponytail.

"What a sweet little girl you are," Rachel cooed, rubbing her breasts and captivating Scarlett.

"Mommy knows you like these," Rachel said, taking Scarlett's hand and leading her back out into the lounge room, enjoying that the plug in Scarlett's ass and the diaper made her walking slightly difficult.

"People are gonna know Mommy," Scarlett whined for the second time as she watched Rachel get her bag and keys.

"Baby," Rachel warned, she loved the look on Scarlett's face. A mix of arousal and fear.

"Get in the car," Rachel said, deciding that would punish Scarlett on the way to the art gallery.

"Mommy!" Scarlett exclaimed, feeling Rachel pull on her overalls.

"Shh, Mommy doesn't want to hear you," Rachel replied, putting her hand down Scarlett's diaper and sliding the vibrator between her pussy lips and turning it on.

"Now they might know," Rachel said, dressing Scarlett once again and beginning to drive away. Scarlett moaned and pawed at herself, wishing that she could be fucked the way she needed and craved.

"I was going to take you to the art gallery, but I don't think we'd make it inside," Rachel said, reaching across and groping at Scarlett's breasts at a red light.

"So this is what I'm going to do, we are going to find a quiet spot, and I'm going to stop the car, open the back door and push you down on the seats and strapon fuck you till your legs give out," Rachel said, beginning to drive off. Scarlett could hardly hear a word she was saying as she was teased, closing her eyes and pushing her head back against the seat, wanting more.

"I'm going to take these hard nipples as a, yes, Mommy," Rachel laughed, knowing that Scarlett was ready and willing to be fucked.

"Oh, Mommy," Scarlett moaned as Rachel unbuckled her seatbelt and got out of the car.

"Get your ass over here," Rachel growled, opening Scarlett's door and pulling her from her seat. Dragging her around to the back seat and pushing her against the leather, Rachel pulled down Scarlett's overalls, ripped off her diaper and took the vibrator and plug from her body. Spat on her strap on and slid it into Scarlett. Putting a paci into her mouth, Rachel pulled out of her just to push back in, Scarlett's arching back and twerking ass encouraging Rachel with every thrust.

"Yes, bounce that ass for me, baby," Rachel moaned, cracking her neck and pushing Scarlett down as she fucked her. Rachel had parked behind a sporting field, a place she knew well, and smiled to herself as she looked down and enjoyed the image that greeted her.

"Such a good girl," Rachel cooed, feeling Scarlett's pussy tighten and then flood, her body shaking. Rachel slowed her pace, knowing that Scarlett would not be able to take much more. Although she had only cum once, Rachel was acutely aware of the psychological toll the kink played on Scarlett.

"Mommy," Scarlett softly said, Rachel, pulling out of her immediately, knowing that she had reached her limit.

"Mommy's here," Rachel said, taking her strap off and collecting their things and putting them in a bag.

"Mommy will sort those out later," Rachel said, putting a new pull up on Scarlett and dressing her once again. Scarlett went to get back in the front seat, Rachel grabbing her arm and pulling her back into her.

"Not so fast," she said, sitting in the back seat of the car and pulling Scarlett onto her lap.

"Open that pretty mouth for Mommy. This is your reward," Rachel explained, Scarlett instinctively beginning to nurse. Rachel stroked her hair, sweeping it out of her face, and smiled as she felt Scarlett grab at her.

"Such a sweet little girl," Rachel affectionately said, closing her eyes and leaning against the seat in contented bliss.

What neither of them realized is that somebody had been watching the whole time. Esther had been following Scarlett from the moment she had left the diner and put a tracer on Rachel's SUV. She had traced them to the field, and had taken photos and of the whole encounter.

"This will fucking show you to say no to me, you little bitch," Esther said as she slowly got up from her hiding position and began to walk away, her sinister plan in motion.

Chapter 11

Esther went home to her modest place in the suburbs and uploaded the content to her laptop, making copies of the photos and printing them out. She didn't have to search very hard to find out the Rachel had saved a tidy little nest egg for herself, and Esther planned to take her for every dollar of it.

"That'll teach you to play with things that are mine," Esther bitterly said as she wrote a note outlining what she wanted.

$50,000 in cash left at 81 Samsom Drive-by Wednesday or the world gets to see just how personal you make your sessions with clients.

"I can hardly wait," Esther said out loud, laughing as she placed the note and photos into a yellow envelope and sealed it. She knew that Rachel had the cash, and she knew that she wouldn't want to be disgraced and lose her license. Esther smiled to herself, poured herself a drink, and went online to find a woman for the night, wanting to celebrate her wicked plan.

"Hey, little one, Mommy's home," Rachel called from the front door. She walked in, saw Scarlett's blocks on the floor, and smiled, knowing that her baby had had a nice day. Rachel had told Scarlett to only focus on her online course, which meant that she was able to work around her own schedule. But what it really meant was that for 5 hours a day she studied, and all the other times, she was Rachel's baby.

"Mommy, I'm in here," Scarlett replied, popping her head up from the couch. Rachel undid the cufflinks from her blouse and walked to the living room, pouring herself a drink from the bar before sitting down on the couch next to Scarlett.

"Mommy, you're silly," Scarlett laughed, snuggling into Rachel, loving the smell of aircon and perfume.

"It was a long day, sweetie. Some people are fucking stupid," Rachel said, annoyed that her clients didn't do what she told them to do.

"It's like, they don't even want to become better, they just want to stay in this toxic little cycle of fucking up their lives," Rachel explained, finishing her drink and exhaling as the liquor burned her throat. Scarlett sat next to her waiting for her to feel better.

"It's okay, Mommy. They are just stupid," Scarlett replied, watching at Rachel turned her head and looked at Scarlett's mischievous smirk.

"You know you're not allowed to use naughty words," Rachel warned. Scarlett knew perfectly well what she was and was not allowed to do, making her giggle.

"But you said it, Mommy," Scarlett replied as innocently as she could. Rachel smiled, tempted, but refusing to take the bait.

"Do you Mommy to punish you tonight? Hey? You've had all day without me, and you're going to try to use my frustration as an excuse to be naughty?" Rachel asked, loving the game that Scarlett had begun. Scarlett giggled, snuggled into Rachel and kissed her neck.

"Maybe," she softly said, getting lost in the embrace that Rachel greeted her with.

"I love you," Rachel whispered, feeling Scarlett's heart skip a beat. Scarlett looked up at Rachel, her surprised face, melting Rachel's heart.

"I don't want to be rough with you tonight," Rachel added, unphased that Scarlett didn't say it back. Rachel knew that it would probably take years before Scarlett felt comfortable to allow herself to feel that deeply. Although she didn't want to therapize Scarlett, Rachel had often found herself analyzing what she was saying or doing.

"Did Mommy make you speechless?" Rachel laughed, seeing her baby girl completely disarmed and nodding her head slowly. Scarlett rested her head against Rachel and closed her eyes.

"You've ruined all my evening plans," Scarlett quietly said, smiling up at Rachel.

"I planned to get you all worked up and for you to take it out on my pussy. But now all I want is to be clingy and needy," Scarlett whined, be secretly delighted that Rachel felt this way about her.

"Maybe Mommy can make up for that?" Rachel asked, deciding that she was going to take Scarlett out for burgers and shakes instead of using her cunt for the evening.

Rachel couldn't sleep. She wasn't sure if it was the amount of take out she had eaten or the fact that her job had become completely unfulfilling. She carefully got out of bed as to not disturb Scarlett and tiptoed through the house to the kitchen to make herself a cup of tea. Sitting on the couch, she sighed as she thought about her life with Scarlett, knowing that she finally felt complete. She got up and opened a window, smiling as she heard the birds beginning their day. She loved taking moments like this. They always seemed like the world was stopping and allowing her to catch up. Putting her mug of tea on the coffee table, she crossed her legs and wrapped a blanket around her shoulders.

I guess this is life now, she thought to herself, closing her eyes just as she heard glass shatter in the kitchen. Gasping and getting up, a knot tightened in her stomach as she heard tires screeching down the street, and she ran into the kitchen to see a yellow envelope wrapped around a brick.

"Rachel, are you ok?" Scarlett fearfully questioned, running around the corner but stopping when she saw the shards of glass covering the floor and the broken window.

"The fuck?" Scarlett added, assessing the situation. Rachel turned around and looked in shock.

"Baby don't come in, there's glass everywhere," Rachel said, wanting to make sure that Scarlett was safe. Rachel bent down to pick up the brick and undid the elastic band that secured the yellow envelope.

"What is that?" Scarlett asked, Rachel, shrugging her shoulders and looking scared and confused. Scarlett hadn't ever seen Rachel look afraid before, and she bit her lip, knowing that now was the time to be tough.

"Here, give it to me," Scarlett said, stepping forward and taking the envelope from Rachel's shaking hands.

"Come and sit down," she added, taking Rachel's hand in hers and leading her back to the couch and placed her mug of tea in her hands.

"Drink this," Scarlett said, wrapping her arms around Rachel, who began to laugh in shock.

"You must think I'm a mess," Rachel said, shaking her head and wiping a tear away.

"Nar, I'm just a little more used to this type of stuff happening than you are," Scarlett replied in a loving tone. Scarlett began to open the envelope, her fingers ripping the paper.

"What?" Rachel asked, seeing Scarlett's face go white. Scarlett handed her the photos, getting up to go to the fridge and get a drink.

"Fuck," Rachel said, reading the note and wondering who would want to do this to her.

"Fuck, alright," Scarlett replied, taking a swing of whiskey straight from the bottle.

"Hey, put that down and come here," Rachel said, seeing Scarlett being to give in to her old vices.

"You know who did this, right?" Scarlett said, the furry in her eyes heightening Rachel's caution as she watched Scarlett pace back and forth.

"Come here, sweetie," Rachel lovingly said, seeing Scarlett shaken and distressed, snapping her out of her own distress, wanting nothing more than to comfort Scarlett. She stopped pacing and looked at Rachel.

"But you do know, don't you?" Scarlett said, sitting next to Rachel and looking at her with those wild and cautious eyes Rachel had first fallen in love with.

"No, I don't. Tell me who you think it was," Rachel said, positioning Scarlett comfortably in her arms.

"It's obvious, that fucking bitch," Scarlett blurted out, annoyed that Esther was still trying to manipulate her life.

"We don't know that for sure," Rachel said, looking over the note.

"I don't even know what I'm meant to say about this," she sighed, passing the note to Scarlett. Reading the note, Scarlett frowned before looking up at Rachel with fear in her eyes.

"She can't be serious!" Scarlett yelled, taking Rachel by surprise.

"Baby, if it is her, she just threw a brick through my fucking window. I think whoever this is, they are pretty damn serious," Rachel angrily replied, startling Scarlett.

"Oh, baby, Mommy's sorry. Come here," Rachel quickly said, changing her tone and holding onto Scarlett firmly, as Scarlett tried to push her away.

"Don't push Mommy just because I made you scared. It's alright," Rachel said, feeling Scarlett relax and begin to cry.

"I know it's scary. But Mommy's here and I'm not going to let anything bad happen to you," Rachel reassuringly explained. Scarlett looked up at her and bit her bottom lip, snuggling into her breasts before closing her eyes.

"I don't have that kind of money," Scarlett whispered, making Rachel smile.

"I do," Rachel cheekily said, deciding that she wasn't going to pay it despite the huge threat to her career. Scarlett sat up, looked at her in surprise.

"Okay but, I still don't think that you should pay it," Scarlett slowly replied, understanding the weight of what she was saying.

"I mean. I don't care about people finding out about me. Like, I don't do anything special. But you! You are going to lose everything you've worked for if you don't pay her, but then if you pay her, what's to stop her from demanding more?!" Scarlett said, getting herself into a frenzy and making Rachel laugh.

"Easy there tiger," she laughed, kissing Scarlett's forehead and thinking.

"We should probably go to the police. Just because I'm not going to pay her, doesn't mean I don't still want her caught," Rachel said.

If I don't pay her, she will probably become more violent. She knows where I live. She might come after Scarlett again, and next time it will be far worse than the first time, Rachel thought, feeling angry as she imagined what Esther would do to her out of spite and revenge for not getting her way.

"I don't really want to stay in the house tonight. What if she comes back?" Scarlett fearfully questioned, looking at Rachel and wanting her to protect her more than she had ever felt in her life. Rachel thought for a moment. It was four in the morning, and the thought of going back to sleep made Rachel feel uneasy as a gush of wind came through the broken window and sent chills down her spine.

"Come on, get your coat, we are going to the station," Rachel declared. She had no desire to see her perfect girlfriend put in any more dangerous and compromising situations, and was fearful that Esther would come back if it was even Esther at all.

"Hello. I'm Victoria," an Amazonian looking woman said, extending her hand to Rachel and then Scarlett.

"Hi, I'm Rachel, this is Scarlett," Rachel said, sitting down on the chair that Victoria gestured toward.

"So, you've had a bit of a rough night?" Victoria said, raising an eyebrow at the yellow envelope that Rachel had in her hands. Rachel looked at Scarlett, who bit her bottom lip and nodded her head.

"Yeah, we have. Um, so, this came with a

brick, and it was thrown through my kitchen window and um," Rachel said, feeling embarrassed about her love of the MDLG kink for the first time.

"It's okay, take your time. But just know that there's no judgment about what's in here," Victoria kindly said, smiling at both Rachel and Scarlett and assessing their dynamic.

"May I?" Victoria asked, Rachel, nodding her head, surprised that she felt so out of control. Usually, Rachel felt in control, her sensual energy empowering herself, and her confidence in her ability always to know how to deal with a situation fueling her fire. But not right now. Right now, she felt as though she was completely stripped of any power she had thought she had, any security she had built around herself, and as she looked at Victoria, any control she had in her life. Scarlett sensed that Rachel was struggling to process what was going on and placed her hand on her thigh. Victoria took the envelope and flicked through the photos, trying not to get turned on. She had sensed that Rachel and Scarlett had some sort of kink to their relationship, but she was pleasantly delighted that their interests were so aligned with her own. She read the note and slowly looked up.

"You've got yourselves a nasty stalker," she said, smiling kindly at Rachel, who found herself blushing, much to her dismay.

"Look, it's okay, if it makes you feel better," Victoria said, tilting her head and shrugging her shoulders and nodding her head in the way that told Rachel and Scarlett everything they needed to know.

"Oh, that actually does make me feel a lot better," Rachel said, deeply exhaling, only realizing that she had been holding her breath at that moment.

"So, now let's nail this person. I hate kink-shaming at the best of times, but this is just cruel," Victoria said, enjoying the change in energy in the room and the way Rachel and Scarlett both relaxed.

Victoria had suggested that they collect their most treasured possessions and go to a hotel for a few days while she investigated. So Rachel and Scarlett had gone back to the house and began to pack their bags.

"I feel like I do this way too much," Scarlett joked, making Rachel's heart hurt.

"I'm sorry, princess," she said, kissing Scarlett's forehead and holding her tightly. Scarlett smiled against Rachel, loving the sensual smell of her perfume and loving embrace. It always made her feel loved, the way Rachel held her. It was the combination of fitting perfectly into her and the placement of Rachel's arms.

"I didn't mean to make you sad," Scarlett replied, realizing that Rachel had no intention of letting her go.

I just never thought my life would be like this. I'm about to potentially lose my career for a girl I've known for the shortest amount of time. I mean, I don't hate it, I just never thought it would happen, Rachel thought, stroking Scarlett's hair and softly laughing to herself.

"You didn't make me sad, baby. I'm just surprised that this is my life. I thought it was getting a bit boring, but I didn't need this level of excitement," Rachel joked. Scarlett felt the familiar knot in her stomach begin to tighten as she thought about the possibility of Rachel leaving her.

What if I just come with too much baggage? She thought to herself, annoyed that just when everything was going right for her, something or someone had to come along and ruin it for her.

I should just go and let Rachel get back to her life. She doesn't need me bringing her down and holding her back by being with me, Scarlett thought, grabbing her bag and waiting for Rachel by the door.

"Ready?" Rachel asked, noticing the fake smile across Scarlett's face.

"Yeah," Scarlett replied, trying to convince

Rachel but failing to do so.

Maybe she's just exhausted from the night, Rachel thought to herself, knowing that that wasn't correct. Rachel didn't have the energy to try and figure out what was distressing Scarlett, but she made a mental note to come back to it, especially if Scarlett stayed faking her happiness.

"Let's go," Rachel added, opening the door just as the emergency repair trades began to work on her window.

Rachel drove to the hotel, checked in, and held Scarlett's hand as they walked to their room, noticing that Scarlett pulled away from her halfway down the corridor.

"I think I'm going to go take a shower," Rachel announced, dropping her bag by the side of the bed and watching as Scarlett looked out over the city from the window. Victoria had told them to stay away for the week, estimating that that is how long it would take her to build a solid case around Esther, so Rachel had booked the penthouse suite for Scarlett and herself.

"Baby?" Rachel questioned, coming over and wrapping her arms around Scarlett, just to have her push her away. Rachel was exhausted, and she had to pause before responding to Scarlett's agitated manner.

"Do you want to talk about it? Do you know the words?" Rachel asked, softening her tone and reaching out to touch Scarlett's cheek. Scarlett's angry eyes glaring back at her made Rachel understand that this was a trauma response.

"I know it feels like bad things are always happening and that you can't get away from your old life, but look at this great place. This is proof that while bad things can still happen because that's life, you are in a position to be less affected by them now," Rachel lovingly explained, seeing Scarlett sigh and become more relaxed.

"I just feel like, if it wasn't for me, you wouldn't have to go through this. And yeah, this is cool, but I only have this because of you. If I was on my own, I'd probs let her do whatever because what would my options be?" Scarlett replied, feeling her eyes lose their anger, just for the sadness she carried to begin to show.

"Well, first of all, my life was boring before you. So if you think that I am giving you up, you are crazy. And second, you're right, but I want you as mine, so just enjoy what I have to give you. Let me spoil and protect and nurture and love on you," Rachel playfully said, making Scarlett smile.

"Why do you even want me?" She asked, shaking her head and shrugging her shoulders.

"Like, I'm not even that good," Scarlett added, making Rachel smile. Rachel took Scarlett's hand and led her to the lounge, sat her down, and looked into her eyes.

"I want you because you trigger in me something that I love. It's that neediness when you feel little that I adore, the way you are always trying to be such a big girl when you aren't little and how when I am sad you come out swinging, wanting to take on the world. You give me joy and peace and love, and I'm not sure what else I could ask for," Rachel said, taking Scarlett by surprise. She wasn't used to hearing those words, let alone directed at her, and their unfamiliarity made her nervous and on edge.

"Come on, let Mommy take care of you, honey. I can tell that you are overstimulated, and I need to get you settled and into bed. Even though it's morning, we had interrupted sleep, and you need a little bit of quiet time to relax and rest," Rachel said, opening her arms to Scarlett, patiently waiting as Scarlett decided if she was going to submit.

"My good girl," Rachel said, feeling Scarlett relax into her, giving herself to Rachel and smiling against her chest, knowing that Rachel was all she wanted. Rachel took Scarlett's hand and led her to the bathroom. Scarlett's eyes were softening as the familiar nightly routine began even though it was mid-morning, and she found herself in the shower, getting gently washed by Rachel's loving hands.

"Do you ever get sick of looking after me?" Scarlett softly asked, her insecurities creeping back in as she looked into Rachel's exhausted eyes.

"What? No!" Rachel said, turning Scarlett around and washing her back.

"It's just that," Scarlett said, stopping when she saw the look on Rachel's face.

"Here. That's enough of that silly talk," Rachel said, pushing Scarlett's paci into her mouth and taking her out the shower and beginning to dry her.

"Stand there while Mommy has a shower," Rachel said, snapping her fingers and smiling as Scarlett blindly obeyed her.

"Oh you know how to please Mommy, don't you," Rachel said, washing herself quickly before getting out of the shower and slapping Scarlett's ass playfully, making her walk back to the bedroom and lay down on the bed, expectantly.

"I know little bunny," Rachel replied, to seeing Scarlett's grabby hands. Quickly diapering Scarlett, Rachel dressed her in her dino onesie and pulled the blankets back, watching as Scarlett scurried under the covers. Rachel put on her panties and climbed into bed, pushing Scarlett's blankie into her chest and laughing at how she grabbed at it as though it was a lifeline.

"Mommy's sweet little girl," Rachel said, wrapping her arms around Scarlett, who quietly snuggled into her.

"Sweet dreams beautiful girl," Rachel whispered, as she felt Scarlett become heavy against her.

Chapter 12

Rachel woke up, the afternoon sun beaming through the cracks in the curtains. Getting out of bed and walking out onto the balcony, she shielded her eyes and felt the cool air against her skin, grounding her.

How should I move on with my life, Rachel thought to herself, sighing and draping her body over the rail.

What do I like the sound of that's not a therapist. Like, what am I even any good at? I could go and retrain, do something different? Maybe I don't even want to stay in this town. We could go anywhere, do anything, she reflected, watching the world continue to spin around her.

I have some really big decisions to make because it isn't just me anymore, Rachel reflected, thinking about how her decision would change not only her life but also Scarlett's.

I wonder if she'd even want to go with me. What if she wants to stay here, what if it all just gets too much for her? Rachel began to think, sitting down on the outdoor furniture and beginning to plan what her new life would entail.

"Hi, do you want one?" Scarlett asked hours later, pouring herself the smoothie she had just made.

"No thanks, baby, it looks yummy, though," Rachel replied. She had gone out that afternoon, taken a walk, and collected the newspaper. Going to the park, Rachel had sat and watched the water features in the pond, read her newspaper, and contemplated her life. She had come home just as Scarlett was waking up, enjoying watching her beautiful girlfriend toss and stir, waking up just as the lights of the city began to flicker and glow.

"I've been thinking about what we should do, little one," Rachel said, folding the newspaper on the kitchen bench and looking at

Scarlett intensely. Scarlett took a sip of her smoothie, raising her eyebrows, sensing the seriousness of the conversation.

"Because I'm not paying that bitch, and I don't care if I lose my license, I want to start a life somewhere new. With you," Rachel said. Scarlett surprised that Rachel was prepared to walk away from everything she had built in the city. It was one thing not to pay Esther. It was another thing entirely to up and run.

"Where would we go?" Scarlett asked, happy to be leaving the city behind.

"I only have a few weeks left of probation, I can't leave before it's over," Scarlett explained, fearful that Rachel would leave her behind. Rachel smirked, stood up and walked around to where Scarlett was standing, wrapped her arms around her and kissed the top of her head.

"Of course we can wait until you have finished that sweetie, I can't imagine leaving without you!" Rachel exclaimed, knowing that setting themselves up in a new town was going to be no small feat.

"We will need to find a new spot, so start thinking about where you want to live little bunny," Rachel called down the hallway as she headed to the bathroom for a shower. Scarlett stayed standing in the kitchen, wondering how she had managed to get this lucky, and walked over to her laptop and began looking at real estate by the beach.

"What if she follows us?" Scarlett asked, curled up in Rachel's arms. Rachel and Scarlett had spent the better part of the last three days looking at properties online and finding a real estate agent. Rachel had decided to rent out her place and had been organizing how to do that with their real estate agent.

"I've never done anything like this before," Scarlett said, feeling overwhelmed by the task. Rachel smiled for her. This was not something that scared Rachel in the slightest, but she could understand why Scarlett found it intimidating.

"Baby, it's really easy. We'll rent out my place, and we will move to a new town, by the beach, and rent a property there to see if we like it," Rachel explained, wrapping her arm around Scarlett, who snuggled into her immediately.

"What's going to happen if we can't find a place?" Scarlett asked, her little voice melting Rachel's heart.

"Mommy's got you, honey, you don't need to worry about not finding a place," Rachel replied, checking the time on her phone.

"Let's stop for the day. What do you want to do?" Rachel asked, understanding that Scarlett needed some time to relax after their day of planning. Scarlett thought, shrugging her shoulders and looking around the space.

"How about Mommy takes you for ice-cream?" Rachel asked, smiling as she saw Scarlett's eyes light up.

"I thought that would get your pretty smile back on your face," Rachel said, standing up and taking Scarlett's hand in hers.

"Don't look at me like that," Scarlett teased, loving how Rachel's gaze landed on her body.

"But you're such a cute, little thing," Rachel sensually said as she lovingly stroked Scarlett's face, making her gasp when she firmly slapped her cheek.

"I want to explore this body before we go, sweetheart," Rachel whispered, taking the pink bunny Scarlett was cuddling and gave her red cheek kisses with it.

"Good thing, bunny is here to kiss you better baby because Mommy isn't going to today," Rachel explained, getting up and going to her bag she had left at the door. She opened the bag, winking at Scarlett, who just giggled and took out two black silk ties and a strap on. Rachel and Scarlett had discussed taking their relationship to the next level and for their sex life to become rougher, and Scarlett was excited to see what Rachel had in store for her.

"I wonder what fun I can have with these," Rachel teased as she dropped the ties on Scarlett's body and began to fasten the harness of the strap on.

"Play with yourself," Rachel instructed, grabbing at Scarlett when she hesitated and leaving red finger marks on her skin, causing her to gasp.

"Oh, you thought I'd be gentle? Silly little girl, you aren't listening to Mommy, are you?" Rachel said, placing her larger hand on Scarlett's neck and squeezing until she was gasping.

"Start playing with yourself little one, you'll want to get nice and wet for Mommy or what I'll do to you will hurt even more," Rachel explained taking Scarlett's left hand and tying it above her head, gently slapping her tits until Scarlett was playing with herself at a pace which satisfied Rachel.

"Good girl," Rachel said, sitting back and stroking the big black dildo she had claimed as her own. Scarlett loved that Rachel always knew how to turn her on, and she giggled, finding it hard to be serious, which made Rachel give her a sideward smirk.

"Oh, you think it's funny, baby?" Rachel said, grabbing Scarlett's ankles and pulling her forward, making her gasp as she felt the tip of the cock against her pussy.

"Not so funny now, is it?" Rachel whispered as she slowly entered Scarlett, being gentle with her and watching for her cues. For the last few days, it had felt like the world was closing in on them, and Rachel cracked her neck as she began to fuck Scarlett, happy to have a release for her frustration. This is what she needed, and as much as she hated herself for using Scarlett as her fuckdoll, she knew that as long as she was gentle, Scarlett would find enjoyment from it as well.

"I'm not going to hurt you, little girl," Rachel said, feeling Scarlett begin to resist her. Rachel knew that she didn't have much time left before Scarlett reached her limit, and she fucked her aggressively with a need and desire she had forgotten she could feel. With the harness from the strap on rubbing against her clit, Rachel came just as Scarlett pushed her away, panting and smirking and satisfied.

"Good girl," Rachel cooed, reaching out to stroke Scarlett's hair, only to be pushed away again.

"Okay, little one," Rachel laughed, understanding what Scarlett needed. Rachel went to the kitchen, made up a bottle, and found Scarlett's blankie before coming back into the room. She took off her strap, lay down on the bed, and let Scarlett snuggle into her, feeling her grabby hands and short breath against her chest.

"There there, Mommy's here," Rachel said, holding Scarlett until her frowning forehead smoothed over.

"That was really fucking close," Scarlett complained, Rachel smirking and letting Scarlett slap at her.

"I know, but it didn't go across the line,

did it?" Rachel replied. She would usually have never let Scarlett be so bratty, but she knew that she had danced close to the edge, and if giving Scarlett a few expectations in her behavior was what she needed to feel better, Rachel was happy to oblige.

"Come on, Mommy needs to get you ready," Rachel whispered, seeing that Scarlett was feeling better. Scarlett's eyes grew wide, and her the innocence of her eyes told Rachel that while she may have needed to use Scarlett like a whore, Scarlett needed her Mommy.

"Oh, has my little girl missed this?" Rachel cooed, seeing Scarlett becoming little before her eyes. Nodding her head, Scarlett battered her eyelids at Rachel as she was diapered and dressed in a baggy pair of jeans and a tight-fitting t-shirt.

"It's cold, Mommy," Scarlett said, shivering as the sun went behind some clouds and the room becoming darker.

"I know, Mommy's got your hoodie,"

Rachel said, sitting Scarlett up and helping her put on her pink hoodie, kissing the top of her nose and making her giggle.

"The ice-cream shop is probably closed by now!" Scarlett whined, making Rachel raise an eyebrow.

"Then I'll come up with a solution, have I ever let you down?" Rachel questioned, liking that the answer was no, as Scarlett shook her head.

Chapter 13

"So, what happens now?" Rachel asked Victoria as she and Scarlett sat in the police station after Victoria had called them in. It had been a week since Esther had tried to blackmail them, and the drop date had come. Victoria had been waiting in place for Esther or anyone to come and collect the money that had been demanded, but with no one showing, it was hard to make a case. Victoria passed Rachel and Scarlett the coffees she had made, before sitting down in her chair.

"Well, the problem is, all the evidence we have for her is circumstantial. We can't actually tie her to anything because there were no fingerprints. The note was printed from a computer and not handwritten so we can't do a handwriting match, and the location was a public place that no one turned up to. There's nothing personal about case that could link it to her,"

Victoria explained, making Rachel and Scarlett annoyed.

"Our plan is to move to the other side of the country and start a new life there. What are we meant to do if she follows us?" Rachel asked, before taking a sip of her cappuccino. Victoria slowly nodded her head. This was the part of the job she hated. When all the circumstances pointed toward one person, but no evidence could tie them to the case.

"I think getting out of here would be a great idea. And if she does send these photos to the psychology board or whoever it is that you answer to, if you don't care about losing your ability to practice, then she's got no power. You can just get on with leading and rebuilding your lives," Victoria explained. She was happy that both Rachel and Scarlett seemed unphased and content with accepting that their lives would never be the same.

"Thanks for all your time," Rachel said, seeing that Scarlett had finished her espresso, extending her hand toward Victoria. Getting up, Victoria walked around the desk, shaking Rachel's hand before shaking Scarlett's.

"I'm sorry that we couldn't get her and lock her up," Victoria replied, knowing that she'd be keeping an eye on Esther for a long time yet.

"Well, that was kind of pointless," Scarlett angrily said as they walked back out onto the street. Rachel laughed, she loved that Scarlett could seem sweet and understanding one moment and bitterly furious the next.

"I know, but it is what it is, so let's just keep doing what we are doing, and hopefully, she won't be able to follow us," Rachel said, shrugging her shoulders and giving a Scarlett a curious look.

"What?" Rachel asked, taking Scarlett's hand in hers.

"You just seem so chill about this when it's taking everything in me not to smash her face in," Scarlett innocently replied, making Rachel laugh.

"That wouldn't be a good idea. This one is much better," Rachel said, taking out the photo of the location they were planning on moving to.

"Oh my gosh, baby, come here and look at this," Rachel laughed from the makeshift desk in the living room. There were boxes all over the house, and she was standing with her laptop on a stack of boxes. The removalist people were going to be arriving at any moment. Esther, at least being true to her word, had sent the photos to the board of Psychology, and as Rachel read their email, suspending her immediately, she laughed. As Rachel laughed from behind the screen, she was happy that she had terminated her license to practice days earlier. Scarlett came out of the bedroom with what Rachel was hoping was the last bag left in there.

"Have you got everything, little one?" Rachel asked Scarlett as she walked over to her.

"Yeah. What is it?" Scarlett asked, gasping

when she read the email from the board of directors.

"Wow, that fucking bitch!" Scarlett exclaimed, happy to be leaving this town behind for good.

"They say they want to investigate, but I honestly can't be bothered trying to convince them that I should stay. It was fun, but I'm ready for something else," Rachel said, closing her laptop screen.

"So, it's official, you have to find a new job," Scarlett laughed, still surprised that somebody would be willing to uproot their entire life just so they could still be together. She had half assumed that Rachel would leave her. After all, it was because of Scarlett that Rachel was in this mess, to begin with, or so she believed. Rachel had a completely different outlook on it, and no matter how many times she tried to convince Scarlett that it wasn't her fault, she refused to believe her. So Rachel had just decided that she was going to have to continue to show Scarlett rather than tell her.

"I already have a few ideas. I'm thinking, maybe opening up a café?" Rachel suggested, just as the removalists arrived.

"We can talk about the plan later," Rachel said, turning to greet them. She and Scarlett had discussed that they would both take a month to settle in before finding jobs. Rachel had enough money tucked aside and was more than happy to use. She had planned a month of full-time baby and Mommy time, and could hardly wait to get set up and begin their fun.

"Well, here's to a new adventure," Scarlett said, watching as the people began to pack their boxed belongings into the back of the moving truck. Rachel winked at her before wrapping her arms around Scarlett.

"Don't worry. Mommy's got you, honey," Rachel replied, knowing that their adventure together was just beginning.

The end... not quite!

To receive your free Baby Fox Coloring In, visit the link:

www.tinamooreauthor.com

Who is Tina Moore?

Tina Moore has enjoyed the lifestyle of a Mommy Domme for several years. She began secretly exploring kink and BDSM in her youth and found her love of being a strict Mommy Domme in early 2000. Tina Moore slowly became more comfortable and confident through making friends in the community and exploring the lifestyle and now openly celebrates being a Mommy Domme to her little.

Before becoming an author, Tina Moore worked in the finance sector, but it was through the encouragement of her current little that she took the leap and wrote her first MDLG book, Nancy's Little One.

From then on, Tina Moore continued to combine her experiences and desires, as well as the sweet and naughty things her baby girl does, to bring you tantalizing and salacious stories about both MDLG and DDLG relationships and the ABDL littles and middles who enjoy them.

Follow her on:
Author Page on Amazon
Instagram @tinamoore.kdp